The Winter Helen Dropped By

A Novel by

W. P. KINSELLA

D1015987

HarperPerennial
HarperCollins*Publishers*Ltd

http://www.harpercollins.com/canada

First published in hardcover by HarperCollins Publishers Ltd: 1995
First HarperPerennial edition: 1996

Canadian Cataloguing in Publication Data

Kinsella, W.P.
    The winter Helen dropped by

1st HarperPerennial ed.
ISBN 0-00-648118-3

I. Title.

PS8571.I57W56 1996   C813'.54   C95-933324-X
PR9199.3.K443W56 1996

---

96 97 98 99 ❖ HC 10 9 8 7 6 5 4 3 2 1

Printed and bound in the United States

Cover illustration: Ron Berg

For my friends, Helen & Ted Zimmerman

The Winter Helen
Dropped By

SECTION ONE

Rat Pie and Fireworks

Chapter One

"Every story," Daddy said, "is about sex or death, or sometimes both."

"What about your baseball stories?" said I, thinking myself more than passing clever.

"You know what the word *phallic* means?" my daddy asked.

"Nope," said I, feeling less clever than I had a moment before.

"Well, y'all come back when you do, and we'll discuss my pronouncement further. No, on second thought," Daddy said, "by the time you understand the word you'll understand the implication."

"Is it something like the women talking about Flop Skaalrud's blatant male aura, when they think no one is listening in?" said I, once again feeling passing clever.

"It is indeed," said my daddy. Then after a pause, during which he scratched his mop of black curls, "So that's what they talk about when they think no one is listening in. Your mama and I will have to discuss that matter."

"Don't tell her you heard it from me."

"Your secret is safe," said Daddy, giving me a large wink.

The area of Alberta where I grew up and spent almost the first eleven years of my life was known as the Six Towns Area. While the town we lived closest to was known as Fark, Fark wasn't big enough to be a town, consisting of only a general store and a community hall and hardly big enough to be called a hamlet. We lived on a farm sixty miles more or less west of Edmonton, Alberta, a distance that in the early 1940s might as well have been six thousand miles more or less west of Edmonton, Alberta, because travel was, as they say in polite society, somewhat restricted.

Only three families in the Six Towns Area owned automobiles, and only three families in the Six Towns Area had telephones, a situation that limited not only travel but communication as well.

None of the families who owned automobiles (though actually only two families owned automobiles; the third owned a dump truck), and not one of the families that had a telephone was our family, the O'Days.

One of the families with a telephone was Curly and Gunhilda McClintock, who, in the process of letting their inherited eight-room house with a cistern and indoor plumbing go to rack and ruin, also allowed their telephone service to be cut off, so while they technically had a telephone, the Telephone Company being too lazy or economy-minded to travel the forty miles from Stony Plain to collect it, that telephone was, my daddy said, dead as Billy-be-damned. I never was too sure who Billy-be-damned was.

Because of a lack of travel and a lack of communication, time didn't mean a whole lot in the Six Towns Area. Daddy claimed he once arrived at Flop Skaalrud's to find Flop holding a piglet up in the air, the piglet eating crabapples off a tree.

"Don't feedin' him like that take up a lot of time?" Daddy asked.

Flop Skaalrud looked at him kind of scornfully, Daddy said, and asked, "What's time to a pig?"

When the roads were good, which was for about two weeks in mid-summer if it wasn't raining and if what we traveled on could seriously be called roads, Daddy and Mama and me traveled to the Fark General Store, presided over by Slow Andy McMahon, all three hundred and some pounds of him, where we bought groceries and the three-week-old *Toronto Star Weekly* which, my daddy said, even though it was three weeks old served to keep our family relatively in touch with reality, unlike some we knew.

The "unlike some we knew" referred to many of our neighbors who either didn't know or had totally forgotten that there was a world beyond the Six Towns Area or their town in particular, be it Fark, Doreen Beach, Sangudo, Venusberg, Magnolia, or New Oslo, none of which were big enough to be called towns but were anyway, because *town* sounded large and *hamlet* sounded small, and *village* sounded only somewheres in between.

Events in the Six Towns Area tended to be measured in years or by seasons rather than by exact dates, an example being the summer Truckbox Al McClintock almost got a tryout with the genuine St. Louis Cardinals of the National Baseball League, which old timers still argue about, some insisting it took place the summer of '45, others willing to bet their life savings that it was the summer of '46. Events I want to tell you about occurred during what became known outside my family as the summer Jamie O'Day damn near drowned, and inside my family as the summer Jamie damn near drowned, though the summer I damn near drowned was actually a spring, so much so that there were little pieces of ice in the water I damn near drowned in, and it was without question the tail end of a spring thaw that all but did me in.

In our family, the summer Jamie damn near drowned was preceded by the winter Helen dropped by, which was preceded by the summer of the reconstituted wedding, preceded by Rosemary's winter.

It will also be helpful to know about Abigail Uppington, the pig who lived in our kitchen; and about Matilda Skaalrud being named in honor of a deceased pig (not Abigail Uppington); and about the infamous Flop Skaalrud's blatant male aura; as well as Earl J. Rasmussen's courting of the widow, Mrs. Beatrice Ann Stevenson, the result of that courtship being the reconstituted wedding, the naming of Lousy Louise Kortgaard, and probably twenty or a dozen other events.

I'm just gonna keep my eyes open, watch, and see if all these stories are, like Daddy says, about sex or death, or maybe both at the same time.

It was actually the summer after the winter Helen dropped by that I truly began to measure the events of my life by seasons, in spite of regularly reading the three-week-old editions of the *Toronto Star Weekly* that were supposed to keep me in touch with reality.

For me, that summer became the summer White Chaps murdered his wife, just as another winter, not the winter Helen dropped by, was remembered for the time when Rosemary, my almost sister, touched my hand.

None of us had ever seen Helen before the winter when she dropped by. "None of us" being the O'Days: me, my father John Martin Duffy O'Day, and my mother Olivia. We lived in a big old house at the end of a trail that was sometimes just a path but was grandly known as Nine Pin Road, a name that didn't have the least bit to do with bowling. It got named long before Mama and Daddy moved there to hide from the Great Depression, named by a man who, Daddy said, had left the *e* off of *Pine* when he wrote to his sister in Norway, so that Nine Pine Road ever after was officially known as Nine Pin Road, even though from our south window you could see a row of nine pines loping across the pasture.

My parents both hailed from South Carolina, though they met in the shadow of Mt. Rushmore, which my daddy says has an array of presidents' faces carved on it. It is in South Dakota, a considerable distance from South Carolina. Daddy was living in South Dakota, a gandy dancer on the railway, Daddy said he was, though he played baseball on the weekends, and when Mama's train slipped off the track, coming to rest in the shadow of Mt. Rushmore, Daddy was on the repair crew sent to put the train back on the track. And, as Daddy says, the rest is more or less history.

Daddy got trapped twice, was how come a boy from South Carolina came to be living in Alberta, Canada; three times if you count marriage as a trap, which my daddy didn't, but which his friends, Earl J. Rasmussen, who lived alone in the hills with about six hundred sheep, and Flop Skaalrud, and Bandy Wicker, the father of my rabbit-snaring buddy Floyd Wicker, and Wasyl Lakusta, who had a good-hearted wife and was one of the Lakustas by the lake, though the lake had been dried up for many a year, did. Earl J. Rasmussen, who was single, had spent the better part of his life courting the widow, Mrs. Beatrice Ann Stevenson, trying to get trapped, and letting her know that he was hers for the trapping.

The widow, Mrs. Beatrice Ann Stevenson, was the poet-in-residence of the Six Towns Area, and could snap off a few lines of Lord Byron or Emily Dickinson or Walt Whitman just in your run-of-the-mill conversation, without being asked to emote or anything of that nature, though Daddy often remarked that it was a shame about Walt Whitman, but that he guessed a few crimes against nature didn't detract from the fact Walt Whitman was a poet who could touch the heart.

The infamous Flop Skaalrud, as Daddy often remarked,

would court anything that twitched. Daddy worded his remarks that way when there were ladies present, but out in the corral he spoke somewhat more directly, as did the women when they were alone in the kitchen of our big old house at the end of Nine Pin Road and didn't know I was scrunched up in my favorite listening position, squeezed between the cook stove and the wood box.

What the women referred to most often when they thought they were alone was the infamous Flop Skaalrud's blatant male aura, that term being the invention of the widow, Mrs. Beatrice Ann Stevenson, the poet-in-residence, though in reality Mrs. Bear Lundquist, who was sixty-two years old, and though she wasn't arthritic moved like she was, was the only published poet in the Six Towns, having had a sixteen-line sonnet published in the *Winnipeg Free Press and Prairie Farmer*. When someone had the indelicacy to mention it, Mrs. Bear Lundquist said she knew full well that a sonnet should have only fourteen lines, but she just couldn't bring herself to cut out that extra rhyming couplet that had occurred to her at the last moment.

The women seemed to be divided into two camps, those who had caught a glimpse (or in one or two cases somewhat more than a glimpse) of the infamous Flop Skaalrud's blatant male aura, and those to whom the blatant male aura was simply the rumor. It wasn't seemly for any of the married ladies to admit to more than the rumor, so they had to rely on the memory and experience of the single ladies, who were few and far between, or the memory and experience of some married ladies who when single had twitched sufficiently to attract the attention of the infamous Flop Skaalrud, which my daddy said required a twitch that would hardly be noticeable to the outside world.

The first time Daddy got trapped, assuming you don't count marriage as a trap, and since Daddy didn't, I won't, was when the barnstorming baseball team he was playing for went more or less bankrupt in Edmonton, Alberta. Daddy, who always was a restless sort, had hooked up with the team when they passed through Butte, Montana, which was where Mama had been heading when her train drifted off the track in the very shadow of Mt. Rushmore, when Daddy had been on the repair crew sent to put the train back on the track.

Daddy had accompanied Mama on the rest of her train trip to Butte, Montana, where her daddy, who was a mining engineer who had worked in South Africa, was settling in to what was supposed to be a permanent job at a copper mine. Daddy settled down in Butte, Montana, and apprenticed himself to learn how to build fine houses, which he did, for a time, until a traveling baseball team passed through in desperate need of a quality third baseman. This was too much for daddy's restless heart, so he joined them and, Mama says, sent money home regular as clockwork until the team, due to a misunderstanding, was scheduled to play a girls' softball team in Edmonton instead of the general high-quality semi-professional baseball teams they usually encountered.

Rather than honor his contract, even if it was a misunderstanding, the owner of the barnstorming baseball team departed for parts unknown, leaving his players to fend for themselves. Daddy was better than average at fending for himself so rather than return to Butte, Montana, which Daddy described kindly as a boil on the posterior of North America, he hired himself out to build fine houses in Edmonton and shortly was able to send for Mama to join him.

Mama and Daddy, to use their own word, *thrived* in Edmonton, Alberta, and Mama went to work for the Ramsay Department Store in their jewelry department and wore a black dress with a white collar, and Daddy built fine houses, and pretty soon they were able to buy a little house of their own, and they discussed having a family, and I became a glint not only in my daddy's eye but in Mama's as well.

There is no reason to believe that Mama and Daddy wouldn't have continued to thrive, except that Daddy got trapped in Edmonton a second time — by the Great Depression.

All of a sudden there were no fine houses to build, and one of the first things folks stopped buying when they discovered that, like everyone else in North America, they were more or less insolvent, was jewelry. Daddy got laid off at his job, and Mama got laid off at her job, and the only things they owned were most of a house and some furniture. Daddy felt it would be immoral to accept Relief, which later came to be known as Welfare, and later still as Social Assistance. Daddy said in his later years that if Relief had been called Social Assistance in the 1930s he might have accepted it and ridden out the Great Depression in Edmonton instead of trading the house for a mostly worthless quarter section of land.

Mama said Daddy never would have taken Relief no matter how much they buttered up the name of it, and he only made his statement about accepting Relief, in retrospect, because he had mellowed with the years.

Mama always said it was a cruel punishment to live in the general area of a town called Fark, when, if our stony and worthless 160 acres had been located just a little differently, the post office would have been Magnolia. Mama regarded Fark as an embarrassment and hated to put it as a return address on an envelope, but, being from South Carolina, she *understood* Magnolia.

Our nearest neighbor was Bear Lundquist, neighbors being relative, as the Lundquists lived about six miles away by road, or trail, or path, or three and a half miles as the crow flies, though no one I knew, including Loretta Cake, who lived in an abandoned cabin with about a hundred cats and was said to have if not magical powers at least the ability to soothe rheumatism, could fly, or even travel "as the crow flies," for to do so would involve crossing muskegs where a person or a horse could sink thigh-deep in moss and water. "As the crow flies" from our house to Bear Lundquist's farm involved crossing Purgatory Lake, which was deep and gray and too cold all year round to even wade into.

According to Bear Lundquist, who was sixty-two years old and arthritic and named because he resembled a Norwegian black bear, the winter Helen dropped by was the coldest in fifty years, and that in a country where every winter was cold, and every summer too for that matter, and fall and spring as well.

"In Alberta," Daddy said, "you take for granted that the weather is always cold even when it's warm, because even when it's warm everywhere else is warmer, so Alberta is still cold even when the weather is warm."

During the winter Helen dropped by, according to the Lundquists, the temperature dropped to 60° below zero, -60° being a point, Bear Lundquist and my Daddy both said, where the sap froze in the puniest kind of trees, causing them to explode, making sounds just like cannons firing. My daddy had fought in the First World War and knew about such things as cannons firing. And I had heard the explosions myself, from inside our house at the end of Nine Pin Road.

The winter Helen dropped by was so cold the coffee froze in the coffee pot where it sat on a counter not fifteen feet from the cook stove, and most of Mama's plants, sitting on the kitchen table not even ten feet from the cook stove, froze stiff as hay-wire, and little sections of stalk could be snapped off like tooth-picks. The kitchen window was decorated in half-inch-thick white frost that looked like the fancy scalloped icing Mama sometimes put on cakes for special occasions.

It was on one of those sixty-below nights, while an evil wind sawed at the straw and manure that chinked the cracks between the logs in our big, old house at the end of Nine Pin Road, and the windows had been frosted up for weeks, and icicles ran down the inside walls from the windows to the floor, and there was a blanket hung over the door to curtail the draft, and each time the wind gusted the blanket puffed out a few inches from the wall, and a horsehide robe stuffed against the crack at the bottom of the door at least partially interfered with the draft that kept our feet and ankles frozen even with heavy socks and boots on, that Helen dropped by.

We were never able to figure what Helen was doing in our part of the country anyway, and we guessed that she had passed at least two other farms to get to our place, and that she had been traveling as the crow flies, because in sixty-below weather the muskegs, and even Purgatory Lake, were frozen, as my daddy said, clear down to China.

One of the farms she passed was guarded by a shaggy German shepherd dog the size of a small pony, who thrived on sixty-below weather and killed coyotes just for sport. My daddy said the only time he'd seen the dog immobilized was when he'd he raised his leg to pee and the stream froze to a nearby barbed wire fence. Daddy said the dog was trapped for a couple of hours until his owner came along and cut the stream with a gas-powered acetylene welder.

The other farm Helen must have passed by to get to our place at the end of Nine Pin Road was occupied by Deaf Danielson, a bachelor, whose hearing, my daddy said, had been left behind in Norway. We had to surmise that Helen was afraid of Hopfstadt's German shepherd dog the size of a small pony, and that Deaf Danielson didn't hear her knocking, though Deaf Danielson's door was never locked, and he would have been delighted at a little company, particularly female company, of a sixty-degree below night with the beginnings of a freeze-the-balls-off-a-brass-monkey Alberta blizzard whining across the plains.

Daddy said that Deaf Danielson spent a considerable amount of money on stationery and envelopes, and even more on stamps, so he could answer ads in the lovelorn columns in the *Family Herald*, the *Winnipeg Free Press and Prairie Farmer*, and *The Country Guide* in an all-out attempt to find a little female company. Daddy and Mama sometimes joked about the letter Deaf Danielson might write — "I am a deaf Norwegian bachelor who last changed his underwear in 1934, and presently sleep with three collie dogs in a converted granary . . . ."

My daddy regarded himself as a better than average card player, something my mama said cost him dearly at times, especially if he got in a game with the infamous Flop Skaalrud or the second-oldest Bjornsen of the Bjornsen Bros. Swinging Cowboy Music-makers who, when he wasn't picking banjo at box socials, community dances, sports days, or ethnic weddings, was a wizard at five-card draw. His wizardry, the second-oldest Bjornsen claimed, had a good deal to do with the rhythms of the cards and the rhythms of the banjo being compatible.

When Helen dropped by, the kitchen table had been moved to within four feet of the cook stove, where whatever part of us was facing the cook stove was hot and whatever part of us was facing away from the cook stove was cold, and Mama's last surviving geraniums were leaning toward the cook stove, which glowed pink as a baby. My daddy was teaching me the basic strategies of seven-card stud, one-eyed jacks and red sevens wild, and since the cold kept Mama in direct proximity to the kitchen table and pink-glowing cook stove, she had joined in the game, even though she had a distinct dislike of gambling.

The stakes were taken directly from Mama's button box, the advertising for Vogue Tobacco in black lettering on the bright yellow tin which was crammed full of colorful buttons of every size and description. We each started with twenty-five buttons. I liked the big black ones that looked like water bugs and some small red ones in the shape of strawberries, and while Mama didn't do much but accept the cards dealt to her, and she primarily let Daddy pick out her best five cards for her final hand, and even though Daddy played every professional strategy he knew — and Daddy knew considerable professional strategy, having acquired a good deal of expertise while fighting in the First World War and while traveling with several semi-professional baseball teams after the war and while working as a gandy dancer on the railroad and playing baseball on the weekends in South Dakota — by the time Helen dropped by and interrupted the game, Daddy had three buttons left and I had four, while Mama had sixty-eight buttons piled in front of her in little stacks of five each.

"That sounds like a knock at the door," Mama said, but Daddy said it was only the wind and nobody in their right mind would be out on a night like this with the temperature -60° at most, for at six o'clock when Daddy went to check the temperature he came back to say the thermometer had burst from the cold, and the little blob of red mercury had trickled down the front of the thermometer (which advertised the M. D. Muttart Lumber Co. of Edmonton, Alberta) like blood.

"Won't be nobody outdoors with a good old freeze-the-balls-off-a-brass-monkey Alberta blizzard whining across the fields," Daddy said.

I was about to agree when my ears caught the sound Mama had heard, and I decided it was indeed a light knock muffled by the door, the blanket, the horsehide robe, and the beginnings of the good old freeze-the-balls-off-a-brass-monkey Alberta blizzard.

Mama was already pulling on the icy doorknob, trying to make the frosty hinges and the frozen door co-operate. She finally did drag it open a foot or two, and a person was indeed outside, one who pushed itself through that two-foot space and came into the kitchen with a cloud of steam and frost and snowflakes.

"Why you poor thing," Mama said, closing the door with one hand and propelling the visitor toward the baby-pink cook stove with the other. "You must be positively froze."

The visitor stopped about three steps into the kitchen and appeared determined not to advance any further. Daddy and me could tell the visitor was a woman, even with the eyelashes thick with frost, and the lower part of her face covered with a scarf, and it took us about another few seconds to discover that the visitor was not only a woman, but an Indian woman.

The visitor kept looking at the floor, and gave the impression she would rather be almost anywhere else but where she was, except maybe out in the sixty-below weather with the beginnings of a freeze-the-balls-off-a-brass-monkey Alberta blizzard whining across the prairie.

"Do y'all speak English?" Mama asked. The visitor let us know by her eyes that she heard, but she didn't speak a word.

"Well, first thing we got to do is get you warmed up," Mama said, and she guided the reluctant visitor to a chair at our oilcloth-covered kitchen table, which must have looked cheery, for the oilcloth was cream-colored with orange and green tea pots in a pattern, six in a circle, like bright flowers blooming on the shiny cloth.

Mama poured coffee for the visitor, while Daddy stoked the stove, and in a few minutes the snow around the visitor's feet began to puddle under the oilcloth-covered kitchen table, which we had moved even closer to the glowing cook stove.

What the visitor had on her feet were full-sized men's toe rubbers stuffed with blue insoles made of something very similar to weatherstripping. The whole package was held together by two ochre-colored sealer rings around each foot.

"It's what poor people wear on their feet who can't afford

regular shoes and boots," Mama had explained to me when I was just little and I had made inquiries about Loretta Cake's toe rubbers and sealer rings when she had come to call, leading eight square-jawed tabby cats on leashes, and looking like, Mama said, she had just escaped from Gypsyland.

Our visitor also had on a pair of overalls, and over top of the overalls a man's shirt, looking like it was made from a patchwork quilt. She also had on quite a few shirts and a raggedy man's parka jacket made of some shiny wine-colored material glazed with dirt. She had a long scarf wrapped around her head two or three times and pulled across her nose and mouth, so what we saw of her was frosted eyelashes and eyes that were deep and dark as a cellar.

The visitor, who I named Helen, though not until late the next day, slept in the kitchen. We started considering what to call her right after we discovered that, as Mama phrased it, she couldn't say boo in English. "I do have a guest room," Mama assured the visitor, even though by then it was obvious that Helen didn't understand a word any of us was saying. "But because of this atrocious weather, the kitchen is the only truly warm place in the house, and I use truly warm advisedly. But at least you won't freeze to death here."

As soon as Helen was partially unwrapped it became clear that she was not too far from being frozen to death. There were deathly white spots on both cheeks, and Mama had me take a table knife and scrape frost off the kitchen window, and she made a little compress of the frost and showed Helen how to hold it to the frostbite.

Mama also showed Helen the flat, white rocks she was heating up in the oven of the old black-and-silver cook stove with the huge warming oven on top and the water reservoir on the side. Mama would wrap the rocks in flannelette and place them in the bottom of my bed, and in her and Daddy's bed, and those rocks would make the beds toasty when we climbed in and would keep our feet warm for most of the night.

Helen accepted a cup of coffee, and seemed delighted that there was any amount of sugar and cream to doctor it with. She scooped in three heaping spoons of sugar, then looked at Daddy as if she expected to be reprimanded, and when Daddy didn't say a word Helen spooned in two more heaps of sugar, then filled the cup right to the brim with the real cream that came from our red Jersey cow, Primrose.

It then occurred to Mama that Helen might be hungry. Mama got a plate of roast pork from the pantry and showed it to Helen, who snatched at the pork like a shoplifter, Mama's quick reflexes moving the plate away from Helen's flashing brown hand.

"You poor thing," Mama said. She handed Helen two slices of roast pork, which Helen crammed in her mouth all at once. While Helen chewed, Mama cut four thick slices of homemade bread, using a long saw-toothed bread knife and holding the bread against her apron-covered belly and cutting towards herself, an action Daddy frequently predicted would some day lead to serious injury. Mama then built two roast pork sandwiches, each one about about four inches thick. Mama slathered the pork with homemade mustard, then peppered and salted it. She poured a glass of milk and sat the whole works in front of Helen, who, as Daddy said, dug right in.

"Poor thing must have been lost for goodness knows how long," Mama said.

Especially in the winter time there were no Indians near the Six Towns Area. Those that tented around in the summer on road allowances or unoccupied land always went back to their reserves come fall and lived in cabins (such as they were, Daddy said) in the winter. There was a reserve about fifteen miles north, somewhere between Cherhill and Glenevis, or maybe Glenevis and Sangudo, and Daddy guessed that must be where

Helen was from, though neither Daddy nor Mama could guess what Helen was doing out in sixty-below weather, with the beginnings of a freeze-the-balls-off-a-brass-monkey Alberta blizzard howling across the plains.

Mama made Helen a bed on the kitchen couch, after pulling it around in front of the pink-glowing cook stove.

It was a couch Mama herself had made in spite of Daddy being the carpenter in the family. Daddy had promised Mama the couch since before I was born, Mama said, and finally when I was about two, she just got a hammer and spikes and some 2x4's, and then she stuffed that frame with red clover and upholstered it in gunny sack, and covered it with colorful blankets and pillows. Until I was old enough not to have an afternoon nap I napped on that couch, which had the big cathedral-shaped radio and the black-and-white-striped Burgess radio battery at the head of it, and I'd listen to all of two minutes' worth of the afternoon soap operas, or as Mama called them, my stories — *The Guiding Light, Ma Perkins, Pepper Young's Family, The Romance of Helen Trent* — before I'd drift off to sleep, no matter how hard I fought to stay awake.

Helen smiled when she saw the couch, and smiled again as she laid one short-fingered brown hand on the gunny-sack surface. I wondered if Indians had furniture in the cabins where they wintered. Daddy said he didn't know, though he did know they didn't have furniture in the tents they lived in along the road allowances in the summer, just blankets and hides and a few cooking pots.

The next morning, Daddy said that the first time he got up in the night to stoke the stove, he found Helen asleep on the floor in front of the oven door. She had wrapped herself and, he guessed, the hot white rock Mama had planted at the foot of her bed, in the blankets.

The next morning the freeze-the-balls-off-a-brass-monkey Alberta blizzard was raging full steam, though Daddy guessed just by sticking his nose out the door that the weather had warmed up to -40°, because the weather always warmed up when it snowed. The sky was solid as fog and close to the ground, and snow was drifted halfway up the east window. Daddy had to put his shoulder against the kitchen door to push it open enough for him to stick his nose out.

Helen seemed surprised and pleased that there was still sugar and cream to put in the coffee, and she poured in sugar until her cup almost, but not quite, overflowed. Helen ate a big bowl of oatmeal covered in cream and sugar, before she tackled four fried eggs and eight slices of toasted homemade bread, and when Mama pushed the four-pound tin of Aylmer's strawberry jam, "No Pectin Added," toward Helen, along with a table-spoon and indicated she should help herself, why, Helen just gave us all a look like she had died and gone to heaven.

Helen was totally surprised by the radio. When Daddy turned the radio on to CJCA in Edmonton to get the grain and cattle prices, Helen looked all around the room trying to see where the music and voices were coming from. The grain and cattle prices were always preceded by a song called "The Red Raven Polka," what Daddy called a shake-a-leg dance number, that the Bjornsen Bros. Swinging Cowboy Musicmakers sometimes played at a box social, barn dance, whist drive, or ethnic wed-ding. I tried to show Helen that the sound was coming out of the cathedral-shaped radio at the head of the couch, and that the power came from the huge black-and-white-striped Burgess battery. Helen finally put her ear up to the front of the radio, then she walked across the room, noting, I guess, how the sound got dimmer as she moved.

"Can't put nothing over on her," Mama said.

Helen smiled like Mama does when she sees a double rain-bow after a thunderstorm.

The blizzard roared on all that day, only Daddy going out to feed the animals, milk the red Jersey cow, Primrose, and carry in more cut wood for the stove.

In daylight, even if the daylight was like dusk all day, I noticed quite a few things about Helen, though it wasn't until after supper that I named her Helen. I guessed Helen was an adult like Mama and Daddy, though pretty young; I guessed eighteen, Daddy said twenty, and Mama was more inclined to sixteen, though she said she'd reserve judgment for a day or so.

Helen was about as tall as Mama, a height Daddy called big as a minute, a minute not being very big at all, only she was what Daddy called big-boned, so she looked a lot larger than Mama. Her hair was long and black as a crow's wing, kind of wild and tangled, her skin was maple-colored and her cheek bones very high. Her eyes were so brown as to be almost black and were wide-spaced and deep-set.

The spots of frostbite on each cheek were angry looking, but she wouldn't have no scars, Mama said, because of us putting the window frost on her cheeks the night before.

Mama and Daddy noticed something I hadn't, something they wouldn't have discussed with me, but since our living space had been constricted by the cold, and since I had a good ear for whispered conversations, I was able to pick up on it.

"Dark as she is, that girl's face is covered with bruises," Daddy said.

"Poor thing. That's probably why she was out," Mama replied. "She must have had to walk clear across Purgatory Lake to get here. It's a wonder she didn't freeze plumb to death."

I decided right after breakfast that it would be my job to teach Helen, who I hadn't yet named Helen, to speak English, but I couldn't quite grasp that a person could not have *any* knowledge of English. I was trying to teach her whole sentences at once and not making any headway when Mama suggested a game, and I got out Snakes and Ladders. By sign language I taught Helen to count the spots on the dice and then she'd count off the same number on the board, and she'd smile and look proud when she landed on a ladder, and she'd giggle like a little girl and whoosh her button down when she landed on a snake.

I tried to get a name out of her. I would point at myself and say "Jamie," and I would point at Daddy and say "Johnny," and I would point at Mama and say "Olivia," and I would point at Helen and wait for her to say something, but the only sound we got from her were giggles when she landed her button on a snake.

Daddy said he figured she understood but just wasn't ready to share her name with us yet. It was about that time I decided, as we were getting to the end of her first day with us, that she should be named Helen. She was partly named for *The Romance of Helen Trent*, the soap opera that asked the question, Can a woman over forty still find romance? and she was partly named for one of my toys, a curly-haired little black animal that I had received from Mama's sister, my Aunt Mary Kaye, the Christmas before, and had already named Helen, for I considered Helen a very exciting name. The toy had deep-set brown eyes and black hair, as dark as Helen's but not as crow-wing shiny.

"We ought to call her Helen," I said, and not hearing any objections, I went through the naming and pointing again, pointing at myself and saying "Jamie," pointing at Daddy and saying "Johnny," pointing at Mama and saying "Olivia," pointing at her and saying "Helen." Helen smiled and giggled just like she'd landed her button on a snake. Still she never spoke a word.

The next few days were some of the happiest of my life, and I bet they were some of the happiest days of Helen's life, too. I was ravenous for a friend, and Helen was willing to be just about whatever I wanted her to be.

*   *   *

Helen, I guess, was surprised about a lot of things at our big old house at the end of Nine Pin Road, which wasn't much of a road at all, especially in the winter, but I guess the thing Helen was most surprised at was that we had a pig living in the kitchen.

We didn't, Mama pointed out that first evening, as she was building roast pork sandwiches for Helen, have a pig living in our kitchen as a rule, unlike some we knew. Helen didn't pay much attention to Mama, but she did laugh the first time Abigail Uppington came tick-tacking across the cold green linoleum from her box under the stove.

Abigail Uppington only weighed about two pounds, and was the runt of a litter that had appeared way too early in the year, having something, Mama said, to do with Daddy's carelessness about keeping the boar and the sows separated. I bet Abigail Uppington didn't weigh half a pound when Daddy brought her in, wrapped in a gunny sack. Mama fixed one of my leftover baby bottles, the rubber nipple stiff and kind of decaying, and fed Abigail Uppington, who at first, like Helen, didn't have a name. It was Daddy who named her, after she'd recovered, and she'd got strong enough to tick-tack across the cold green linoleum from her box.

"She acts like she owns the place," Daddy said.

Abigail Uppington was a character on a radio show called *Fibber McGee and Molly*, a character who was kind of like the widow, Mrs Beatrice Ann Stevenson, the artsy-craftsy person of her town, Wistful Vista.

Helen and I played with Abigail Uppington, and Helen laughed and hugged the little pig, and Mama pointed out, even though Helen didn't understand a word and couldn't, as Mama said, say boo in English, that pigs were extremely clean animals, cleaner than dogs certainly, and possibly even cleaner than cats. One of Mama's chief worries in life was that someone, anyone, would think she was a dirty housekeeper.

Mama even got out some doll clothes she'd saved from when she was a girl, and she took a minute out of her work while her and Helen tied a pink bonnet on Abigail Uppington, and when Daddy came in from tending the animals he thought Abigail Uppington in a pink doll's bonnet was about the funniest thing he had ever seen, and he laughed his laugh which was really a guffaw and could never be mistaken for anything else.

I got out a jigsaw puzzle, which Mama and I both decided would transcend the language barrier. Helen caught on real quick and giggled every time she found a piece that fit, though the way she looked at me and the puzzle, which was of a group of dogs sitting about a table playing poker, the two English bulldogs cheating by passing cards to each other, I bet she wondered *why* we were doing what we were doing. Mama said she expected Helen spent most of her time just foraging for a livelihood and didn't have time for putting pink bonnets on pigs or passing the time with jigsaw puzzles.

On the night *Fibber McGee and Molly* came on the radio, sponsored by Johnson's Wax of Racine, Wisconsin, Daddy pointed to the radio when Abigail Uppington came to call on Fibber McGee, and said "Abigail Uppington," and then pointed at the pig Abigail Uppington who was on Mama's lap drinking from my baby bottle.

I don't think Helen understood, but she did like the radio and laughed whenever Daddy laughed, which was about two to one for every time me and Mama laughed.

When *Fibber McGee and Molly* was over Daddy told Helen the story of how Matilda Torgeson of the Venusberg Torgesons was named for a dead pig. Seemed that Anna Marie Torgeson, when she was about seven years old, had adopted a runt of the litter, just like Abigail Uppington, only Anna Marie Torgeson named her pig Matilda. The runt survived and prospered, but Anna Marie's daddy, Gunnar Torgeson, was a practical man, and when it came time for Matilda to go to market, off she went, in spite of Anna Marie's wailings and weepings. To ease her pain, Anna Marie's mama promised that Anna Marie could name the next critter born on the farm Matilda.

"Well," Daddy said, "the next critter born on the farm was Anna Marie's little sister, so the new little sister got named Matilda, in honor of a dead pig.

"It's a good job Anna Marie didn't name her pig Runty or Big Snout," Daddy said, and guffawed again.

Helen turned out to be a wonderful playmate. She enjoyed playing with my stuffed toys and with my motor cars, and she was particularly taken with a tiny baby with celluloid arms and legs wearing a blue polka-dot dress. That tiny baby had a key in her belly, and when she was wound up she crawled across the floor, making a kind of crying sound just like a real baby. Helen hugged that little baby and she leaned way back in her chair and let the baby climb right up her from her waist to her chin.

While I had been caught once being totally unobservant, I wasn't about to get caught a second time, and it was me who pointed out to Mama and Daddy that Helen was pregnant.

I made sure of my ground before I brought the subject to Mama and Daddy's attention. I cuddled the little mechanical baby and rocked it in my arms, and looked at Helen, and then I pointed at Helen's stomach and pointed at the baby, and Helen smiled and pointed at her stomach and pointed at the baby. I had noticed that under all the layers of shirts and overalls that Helen's belly was round and ripe, and her hips were wide. Just to confirm my opinion I got out a book that had pictures of babies in it, and showed them to Helen. Helen patted her belly and pointed at the picture of the baby, indicating with no possibility of misinterpretation that she was building a baby inside her, though the baby she pointed at was pink as a rose petal, with blue eyes. I wondered what Helen thought of when she dreamed of her baby, I wondered if she dreamed of a blond, blue-eyed baby, pink as a rose petal.

"I do believe you're right," Daddy said, after I pointed out that Helen was pregnant, and Mama also agreed and went and got some of my old baby clothes, and some of the new baby clothes that she had created or acquired during the time she was pregnant with my almost sister, Rosemary. And Helen smiled some more and picked out two pink baby dresses, and a yellow blanket, and put them on top of her dirt-glazed parka so she wouldn't forget to carry them away when she left.

Leaving was another matter. The good old freeze-the-balls-off-a-brass-monkey Alberta blizzard just raged on and on. The snow drifted up until the east window was blocked entirely, and the wind was so strong it blew the chickadees right off the branches of the chokecherry tree outside the west window and bounced them off the glass as they tried to pull the dried fruit off the frozen limbs.

Helen continued to eat like she'd never had home-cooked food before, while Mama taught her to wash dishes and set the table and empty the ashes from the cook stove, and, Mama said, Helen caught on quick.

I took to reading to Helen from story books I had outgrown. I read her nursery rhymes and Mother Goose stories, showing her the pictures at the same time, and even if Helen didn't understand the words she was able to catch the rhythms, and she clapped her hands when the big bad wolf huffed and puffed and blew down the houses of the three little pigs. And Helen pointed at the little pigs and she pointed at Abigail Uppington, and I clapped my hands and Helen reached right over and put her arms around me and hugged me.

Helen particularly liked the rhyme about the three little kittens who lost their mittens, and she had me read that one over and over until I got plumb tired of it, and Daddy said now I knew what I had been like as a little kid and how he and Mama had read those books to me until they were engraved in their brains. The three little kittens rhyme ends with "There'll be rat pie for supper tonight," and there was a picture of an ordinary-looking pie but for a rat's tail sticking out of it. Helen, whenever we got to that part, would cover her mouth and shake her head. I tried to explain that the rat pie was for cats and not for humans, but I'm not sure Helen ever understood.

"Can't we keep her?" I asked Mama. "She likes it here and she ain't no trouble, and she'll catch on to talking in a few days."

"Helen ain't a pet," Mama said. "She'll likely want to get on home soon as the blizzard lets up."

Which she did. But not before she said her first words. At supper on the third night we had apple pie. Mama had me go to the cellar and get a quart of preserved apples and she hammered out a crust and placed this big apple pie on the oilcloth-covered kitchen table right after we'd finished a feed of side pork and eggs.

"Rat pie!" I announced.

And for just one instant Helen believed me. She had her hand half way to her mouth when she realized I was teasing, and she smiled and shook her head, and then she said "rat pie," and pointed at the pie and laughed like a little girl.

"Helen talked," I said.

"Indeed she did," said Mama. We all raised our cups to Helen and said "Rat pie," and laughed like maniacs.

"In the middle of a blizzard people tend to be amused by relatively simple things," Daddy said.

I know Helen would have been talking with us like a regular person in just a few more days, but late that evening the blizzard died down, and deep in the night a chinook swept in, and by morning the powder-dry snow was soggy and the air was warm and moist, and Daddy said he guessed it had gone from -40° to almost 40° above.

Helen had her parka on when she sat down to breakfast and we could tell she was anxious to get to wherever she was going. Mama packed her a big lunch with four meat sandwiches and a quarter of an apple pie, and Mama packed up a whole bundle more baby clothes and forced them on Helen. I gave Helen my picture book with the story of the three little kittens, and said "rat pie," as I gave it to her, and Helen said "rat pie," as she accepted it. And we all laughed like maniacs.

Daddy and me and Benito Mussolini, my cowardly dog, all walked Helen as far as the barn, where Daddy sent me in to pick up another gift for Helen, which she accepted, and Daddy shook her hand and I hugged her, and she went on her way. No matter how hard I tried I couldn't keep big tears from rolling down my cheeks.

"I know about how you feel," Daddy said. "You've had your first taste of being a parent. In spite of Helen being an adult, expecting a baby of her own, she was out of place and more or less helpless while she was with us. It's awful easy to love someone who's helpless."

Chapter Two

The summer before the winter Helen dropped by was not named for one specific event, but for several, unlike the summer following the winter Helen dropped by, which was forever after known as the summer Jamie O'Day damn near drowned except in our family where it was simply the summer Jamie damn near drowned, though the season really was spring and there was ice in the water I damn near drowned in.

The summer before the winter Helen dropped by was known in some circles as the summer Earl J. Rasmussen and the widow, Mrs. Beatrice Ann Stevenson, officially tied the knot, and then officially retied it in a reconstituted wedding, and in other circles as the summer my daddy took on the bureaucracy to straighten out the life of Lousy Louise Kortgaard.

Both of those events had their beginnings, I believe, at the July 4th Picnic and Sports Day at Doreen Beach, it being the turn of Doreen Beach to host the annual July 4th Picnic and Sports Day, Fark having hosted it the year before, and Sangudo

28

being scheduled to host it the next summer. The July 4th Picnic and Sports Day was the high point of the social season in the Six Towns Area, a fact often pointed out by the widow, Mrs. Beatrice Ann Stevenson, our poet-in-residence, and Mrs. Edytha Rasmussen Bozniak who, as Mama frequently said, was lurking in the wings waiting to become *the* person of artistic integrity in the Six Towns Area, should the widow, Mrs. Beatrice Ann Stevenson, ever falter. Mama said marriage to Earl J. Rasmussen, who lived alone in the hills with about six hundred sheep, would be considered by many to be faltering.

July 4th, while admittedly an American holiday, was what was celebrated in the Six Towns Area of Alberta. The first of July was celebrated in Canada as Dominion Day, but, Daddy pointed out, and so did people like Earl J. Rasmussen and Bandy Wicker, both of whom had emigrated from the United States, and Wasyl Lakusta and Deaf Danielson and Adolph Badke, who had emigrated respectively from Ukraine, Norway, and Germany, that everyone had come to Canada to be free, which they were, but they resented that Canada wasn't really an independent country, and each and every one of them resented that the King of England was officially the head of state in Canada, and that Canadians sang "God Save the King" at official celebrations, and didn't have a real flag but one with the English flag, the Union Jack, sitting in its corner and some kind of gold lion or griffon that made it just reek of royalty, something every one of them immigrants had come to North America to get away from. So no one much objected when the official celebration in the Six Towns Area took place on July 4th. Loretta Cake, who lived in an abandoned cabin near to Doreen Beach with about a hundred cats, said something about it being unpatriotic, and so did a family named Baskerville lived up Glenevis way. He had been a major in the British Army and walked around wearing a monocle and hired Indians to work his land because he described himself as a gentleman farmer. But it was generally agreed that English people didn't know how to have a good time, and that was the deciding factor.

"If the English was running the celebration," my daddy said, "we'd all have roast mutton, give a hip-hip-hurrah for the King of England, and go to bed early."

Earl J. Rasmussen said he didn't see a thing wrong with folks eating mutton, and if more did why he'd make a better living.

Daddy said, "Mutton tastes like wool," and that Earl J. Rasmussen should have settled in England where people eat sheep, wool and all.

One of the many highlights of the July 4th Picnic and Sports Day was the fireworks display, which came at dusk. The fireworks had to be ordered, something that was usually done in March or April, or whenever the annual spring flood of Jamie O'Day Creek, which my daddy had named after me, receded sufficiently for either Daddy or Earl J. Rasmussen or Bandy Wicker to ride horseback as far as Fark and accompany Curly McClintock in his inherited dump truck, along with Curly's son, Truckbox Al McClintock, who once almost got a tryout with the genuine St. Louis Cardinals of the National Baseball League, riding shotgun, to Edmonton where the fireworks were ordered at the Acme Novelty and Carnival Supplies store, on 114th Street, just north of Jasper Avenue.

Acme Novelty and Carnival Supplies store also rented merry-go-rounds and carnival games of skill, like over-and-under and ring toss and the one with cement milk bottles and soggy baseballs and a genuine roulette wheel that had once spun in front of the crowned heads of Europe. Acme was owned by a Mr. Prosserstein, who, it was rumored, was Jewish, though no one from the Six Towns Area, even my daddy, who had traveled widely, had to the best of their recollections ever encountered anybody who was Jewish. Mr. Prosserstein did drive a sharp

bargain, they said, but not an unfair one, and he was dark com-
plected, Daddy said, and did speak with an unfamiliar accent,
and was disinclined to work on Saturdays, all of which considerations pointed to the likelihood that he was Jewish.

The widow, Mrs. Beatrice Ann Stevenson, whose only knowledge of Jews came from a play by William Shakespeare, pointed
out that Seventh Day Adventists didn't work on Saturdays
either, and that maybe Mr. Prosserstein was a Seventh Day
Adventist. She suggested that they carry a roast beef sandwich
with them and offer it to Mr. Prosserstein, and if he turned it
down why it would prove he was a Seventh Day Adventist,
because Seventh Day Adventists were vegetarians.

Daddy said that a roast pork sandwich would be equally
enlightening, because if Mr. Prosserstein refused, it would prove
he was Jewish because Jews didn't eat pork.

Mama said that the only thing a refusal of either beef or pork
would prove was that Mr. Prosserstein wasn't hungry, and what
did it matter if he was Jewish or Seventh Day Adventist anyway?

Nobody could answer Mama that and the subject got
dropped.

Daddy told me Mr. Prosserstein had offered in strict confi-
dence that for a small extra fee he could line them up with a
freak show consisting of a bearded lady, a fat man, and a strong
man who could lift a plowhorse off the ground with only one
hand, or for an even larger fee he could supply dancing girls
along with their own tent and a saxophone player. The men of
the community called a Farmers Union meeting in our kitchen
in order to discuss the dancing girls, but it was decided that the
opposition from the women of the Six Towns Area would be
too strong if the offer were brought into the open, and if the
show were presented surreptitiously, it was agreed that reprisals
by the women of the Six Towns Area would be too loud and too
lengthy for the small amount of pleasure derived.

Several times a year, whenever the subject of fireworks came up, Bandy Wicker would have to tell the story of how in his home town of Odessa, Texas, the July 4th fireworks display once took on a certain air of tragedy.

"My cousin Verdell had come home especially for the fourth of July celebrations," Bandy Wicker said. "Cousin Verdell, he'd been working way out in Deaf Smith County, doing something simple enough for his mind to grasp. Cousin Verdell was kind of like a turkey, you had to keep his nose pointed down during a rainstorm, or he'd have stared at the sky until he drowned.

"What happened," Bandy Wicker went on, "was that the mayor of Odessa, Texas, touched a match to the fuse of the rocket held in place by the length of sewer pipe, and a whole passel of people prepared to ooooh and aaaah at Old Glory lighting up the night-time sky for a guaranteed thirty seconds.

"People waited and waited, and the mayor walked back and made sure the fuse of the rocket in the upright sewer pipe was burning. We all gathered around the rocket when it appeared that the fuse had burned itself both out and off. No one studied the problem more closely than Cousin Verdell, who was leaning directly over top of the rocket and peering down at goodness knows what.

"It was about this time the rocket decided to fire itself off, an unfortunate occurrence because Cousin Verdell was still standing directly above the rocket, as if it had some mystical significance. The rocket, filled with Old Glory, including forty-eight silver stars, one for each state, terminated Cousin Verdell, instantly.

"While there was a certain degree of tragedy involved in Cousin Verdell's being called to his reward, it was agreed that he had lived longer than anyone that dumb had a right to."

My daddy would always top Bandy Wicker's fireworks stories with his baseball stories. My daddy had a million baseball stories.

"Folks around Doreen Beach," he'd start off, "were not noted for their baseball prowess. For several years there were only eight men in the Doreen Beach district who could play any kind of baseball. To show the lengths folks around Doreen Beach would go to to field a team, one Sunday when there had been a Holy Roller church service at Doreen Beach Community Hall, the ballplayers hid Brother Bickerstaff's horse until he agreed to be their ninth player, while on another occasion a group of men rode over to Loretta Cake's cabin, where she lives with about a hundred cats, with the intention of convincing her to stand in right field as the ninth body on the Doreen Beach White Sox baseball team."

Loretta Cake, who was at best considered eccentric and at worst somewhat mad, confided to Mama on one of the infrequent occasions when she dropped by our house leading eight square-jawed tom cats on leashes and dressed to resemble a middle-aged Englishwoman playing Sheena, Queen of the Jungle, that she harbored secret rape fantasies, a confession that embarrassed my mama no end, and, Loretta Cake went on, she felt that her secret fantasies were about to be fulfilled when she peeked out her window of a Sunday morning and saw several young men on horseback, wearing mackinaws and slouch hats, resembling for all the world the Dalton gang.

I thought Loretta Cake's confession to be somewhat humorous, hearing it scrunched up in my favorite listening place between the wood box and the cook stove, as I didn't understand the implications, rape not being a dinner-table topic of conversation in our household, or any household in the Six Towns Area, except possibly that of Loretta Cake and her cats.

The reason I didn't understand the implication was because, the summer before, one of the Osbaldson boys from around New Oslo had planted five acres of rape, which grew the most beautiful yellow color I had ever seen, looking for all the world like a five-acre canary squatting in the midst of the Osbaldson boys' green grazing land.

I thought Loretta Cake's rape fantasies humorous on two levels, one being that Loretta Cake, even if she did go around dressed like Sheena, Queen of the Jungle, should have secret fantasies about a field of yellow grain; and two, that Loretta Cake's secret fantasies about a field of yellow grain should embarrass my mama.

I did not have the sense to keep my mouth shut, so of a Sunday morning on our way to a Sports Day and Picnic at New Oslo, as we were passing by the Osbaldson boys' five-acre-canary-sized field I suggested I pick a bouquet of the rape to present to Loretta Cake when she appeared at the New Oslo Sports Day and Picnic.

Across the buggy seat, Mama and Daddy exchanged some of the strangest looks I ever saw them exchange in their entire life together, before Daddy explained to me that the word *rape* had more than one meaning. By the time he finished I wasn't sure exactly what the other meaning was, except that I had no call to know of it until I was at least twenty-one and living on my own.

My wanting to take a bouquet of rape to Loretta Cake found its way into letters to Mama and Daddy's relatives in Montana, South Carolina, and South Dakota, and the ears of the widow, Mrs. Beatrice Ann Stevenson, which was the same as broadcasting the story on CJCA in Edmonton, the radio station most available in the Six Towns Area to those of us who owned radios.

The story passed through the crowd at the New Oslo Sports Day and Picnic even quicker than pinkeye, and I got my hair rumpled and my cheek tweaked for most of the afternoon and evening, though no one ever mentioned to Loretta Cake, who was there, big as life and twice as ugly, Daddy said, why everyone was rumpling Jamie O'Day's hair and tweaking Jamie

O'Day's cheek, for a secret is a secret, and Loretta Cake's secret rape fantasies were safe with everyone in the Six Towns Area.

Even though the proposition by the Doreen Beach White Sox did not match her secret fantasy, Loretta Cake agreed to accompany the Doreen Beach baseball club and to sit behind the saddle of the handsomest ballplayer, who, she said, bore a startling resemblance to the outlaw Wade Dalton. Just as she was mounting the horse it stepped on the tail of one of her cats, and the screech the cat set off made the handsomest ballplayer's horse rear and throw Loretta Cake onto her posterior and the handsomest ballplayer onto his neck, both on the ground.

The handsomest ballplayer, who bore a striking resemblance to the outlaw Wade Dalton, was a Kortgaard, one of Lousy Louise Kortgaard's big brothers, and he lay unconscious for some time before being carried to the ball field draped over the back of his horse, while Loretta Cake, cuddling one of her cats, sat in the saddle. His teammates propped the unconscious Kortgaard up on a stack of blankets at third base and began the first game of the tournament against an all-Indian team from the reserve at Lac Ste. Anne.

However, after there was only one out and two runs in, the umpire visited third base, waved his mask and then his cap and then his bare hand in front of the unconscious Kortgaard's face and, getting no reaction, declared the unconscious Kortgaard ineligible and suggested that someone should send a message to Curly McClintock over at New Oslo to head for Doreen Beach and cart the unconscious Kortgaard to the hospital, forty miles away in Stony Plain. Even with Loretta Cake and her cat in right field, the Doreen Beach White Sox had only eight players and were required to forfeit the game, thus cutting short Loretta Cake's career as a right fielder.

*   *   *

On the Saturday before the Sunday when the fourth of July celebrations were to be held at Doreen Beach, Daddy and I accompanied Curly and Truckbox Al McClintock to Edmonton in Curly's inherited dump truck in order to pick up the fireworks from Mr. Prosserstein at the Acme Novelty and Carnival Supplies store. The cab of the dump truck smelled of grease and exhaust fumes, and the four of us sat ankle-deep in mufflers, crankshaft parts, and expired plugs, points, and condensers. Curly McClintock, who was slow moving and slow thinking, and who, Daddy said, was built so close to the ground his knuckles dragged, had created a son in his own image, except that Truckbox Al's facial features resembled his mama, the youngest and most bulldog-faced Gordonjensen girl. My own daddy in his bib-overalls, black mackinaw sweater my mama had knitted him, and tweed cap, certainly appeared large to me, though my daddy preferred *burly* to describe his physical build.

The Acme Novelty and Carnival Supplies store was exactly as I had imagined heaven, full to the eyeballs, as Daddy put it, of every geegaw know to man and a few that weren't. There were fake false teeth that wound up with a key and chattered when set on a table; a whole section with nothing but stuffed toys, another with nothing but box games, and a jewelry section with genuine diamond rings for as little as five dollars each.

I was allowed to carry one of the two boxes of fireworks to the truck, and while the box was large and had the name "Acme Novelty and Carnival Supplies" stenciled on its side, it didn't weigh but ten pounds at maximum. I had somehow always thought of fireworks as being heavy.

At the baseball tournament at Doreen Beach, there were four teams: New Oslo Blue Devils with Truckbox Al McClintock playing right field and wielding a big bat, the all-Indian team from the reserve at Lac Ste. Anne — the Indians from Lac Ste. Anne were always able to raise a team, Daddy said, because they had about two thousand people on the reserve, whereas the communities in the Six Towns Area often had difficulty coming up with nine live, or semi-live, players — the Sangudo Mustangs, and Doreen Beach, who, since they were the host team, had made a monumental effort to come up with a full contingent, which they did, without even having to call on Loretta Cake. The unconscious Kortgaard, having eventually recovered from landing on his neck in Loretta Cake's front yard, had gotten himself married to the second-oldest Venusberg Yaremko girl, who was built like a brick backhouse and who, when viewed from the side, had a startling resemblance to a pig, a statement made in all kindness, my mama said, because, swear on a stack of Bibles, it was true. Now, the second-oldest Venusberg Yaremko girl was taller than the unconscious Kortgaard whether standing up or lying prone, and probably also stronger, for she had once punched out one of the Dwerynchuk twins, either Wasyl or Bohdan, no one was sure which, after a dance and box social at New Oslo, where raisin wine, dandelion wine, homemade beer, and good old bring-on-blindness, logging-boot-to-the-side-of-the-head home brew had been consumed, a good deal of it by the second-oldest Venusberg Yaremko girl, who, it was said with some admiration, could drink like a man.

Outside the New Oslo Community Hall, next door to the Christ on the Cross Scandinavian Lutheran Church, the second-oldest Venusberg Yaremko girl had worked through the stages of name calling, shoving, fist-fighting, and genuine altercation, finally kayoing one of the Dwerynchuk twins, either Wasyl or Bohdan, with a punch, Daddy said, like Joe Louis used to knock out Max Schmelling.

Well, the long and the short of it was that the second-oldest Venusberg Yaremko girl, wife of the unconscious Kortgaard, became permanent right fielder for the Doreen Beach White Sox, and, over a period of two years, they entered seven consecutive sports-day baseball tournaments until one October their pitcher lost his pitching arm in a threshing machine and set the Doreen Beach White Sox to rebuilding.

My daddy admitted there was a certain reluctance to accept a team permanently composed of men and women, though the precedent had long ago been set, and no one ever complained. Mrs. Bear Lundquist, who was sixty-two years old and though she wasn't arthritic moved like she was, had played first base for the Sangudo Mustangs for more years than most of the players had been alive, plus Mrs. Bear Lundquist was inclined to bring home-made apple pie to each tournament she played in, enough for both the Sangudo Mustangs and their opponents, and while she was a passable hitter, a lifetime .240 average my daddy said, she was also known to keep her fancy work in the big old trapper glove she wore at first base and was known to knit and purl a few stitches while a pitching change was being made. One time with a runner on first, after fielding a one-hopper, Mrs. Bear Lundquist threw her ball of crocheting yarn to the second baseman instead of the baseball.

"What the heck's that?" the second baseman bawled.

"Pink variegated," Mrs. Bear Lundquist replied. "Ain't it just the prettiest shade you ever seen?"

However, the second-oldest Venusberg Yaremko girl was a different matter. "Except," Daddy said, when him and several friends was gathered out by the corral, "that she lacks the one piece of equipment that makes Flop Skaalrud famous, she is a man through and through."

"A batting average of .302," said Earl J. Rasmussen, "and she fields third base like a twelve-foot chicken-wire fence."

"I reckon she can pee against the hen house wall with the best of us," said Bandy Wicker, that being the highest praise anyone was ever apt to receive from Bandy Wicker. The others present said they had to agree, and with that acknowledgement the second-oldest Venusberg Yaremko girl was accepted as a regular player at sports days, picnics, tournaments, and fourth of July celebrations in the Six Towns Area.

The fireworks were shot off from the outfield at Doreen Beach, before the Bjornsen Bros. Swinging Cowboy Musicmakers set up in the community hall to play for the dance, which would be interrupted by a box social.

Of course it wasn't really dark enough to shoot off fireworks, but what with the baseball games being over (the Doreen Beach White Sox won the tournament with an extra-inning 12–11 win over the all-Indian team from the reserve at Lac Ste. Anne), and with the three-legged, the sack, and the wheelbarrow races having been run, and two tubs of vanilla ice cream Curly McClintock had trucked out from Edmonton that very morning all scooped onto cones and eaten up, there was nothing left but to watch the fireworks and get to the dancing, so with children bawling and whining and squalling, and being tired and dirty-faced, fretful and downright testy, it was no wonder the mothers convinced Bandy Wicker to begin setting off the fireworks while it was barely dusk.

While both Daddy and Bandy Wicker described the rockets of their youth as shooting upward with a whiz and whirr through the blue-black nighttime sky, sending up spumes of red, green, blue, or silver stars that hung in the sky, burning out slowly and leaving behind their images in smoke wavering like moon shadows, the rockets at Doreen Beach on the night of the fourth of July would fire off with a certain whiz and whirr, but when they got up in the sky there would be a loud bang and a few sickly-looking stars would dribble toward the earth, none of them lasting much longer than your run-of-the-mill firefly. The crowd was prepared to ooooh and aaaah at the spectacular bursts of color in the night-time sky, but the sound that emanated as the few sickly-looking stars dribbled toward the ground was more like a groan.

Bandy Wicker, who, in spite of his propensity to self-injury, had been formally entrusted to light the rockets in the outfield of the Doreen Beach baseball grounds, blamed the poor performance on the fact that the fireworks had been manufactured in China, rather than Juarez, Mexico. He said that if Mexican fireworks were inferior it was possible to take revenge on the Ortega Bros. Fireworks Company of Juarez, Mexico, but he didn't see no way we could take revenge on a company in China whose name wasn't even printed in English on the rockets.

Bandy Wicker also wanted to know if we had got a guarantee from Mr. Prosserstein of the Acme Novelty and Carnival Supplies store that our money would be refunded if the rockets didn't fire off properly.

My daddy, who was pushing the little wire legs of the rockets into the ground so they would be properly pointed at the sky and not at the crowd congregated on the bleachers behind home plate, hmmmed a little, stalling for time, hoping some of the rockets would fire off beautiful bursts of colored stars and forestall further criticism. After a few more rockets had succeeded only in making a large bang and dribbling a few sickly-looking stars toward the ground, Daddy hawed a little, as well as hmmming.

"Guess next time we'll have to send a real man to do the job," said Bandy Wicker, lighting a couple more rockets, one of which set off with a whiz and whirr, and one of which didn't.

What folks didn't notice was that the few sickly-looking stars that dribbled toward the ground carried a certain amount of firepower, and that most of the sickly-looking stars dribbling to earth behind the bleachers tended to set the grass a-smouldering.

So little rain had fallen that Brother Bickerstaff of the Holy, Holy, Holy, Foursquare Church of Edson, Alberta, had held a holy roller religious service that very morning in the Doreen Beach Community Hall to extract rain from the high, dry, blue Alberta sky by means of prayer.

Folks did not notice the smouldering grass, or the little fringe of burning grass that crept toward the bleachers, and toward the Doreen Beach Community Hall, and toward the Doreen Beach General Store, and toward the one and only house in Doreen Beach, the residence of Torval Osbaldson and his wife, Tillie, retired farmers who had moved to Doreen Beach to enjoy the hustle and bustle of town life in their declining years. And folks did not notice the fire creeping toward Slow Andy McMahon, all three hundred and some pounds of him, where he sat with his back against a large cottonwood tree, dozing fitfully and eating from several boxes of prepackaged McGavin's Bakery donuts, and a four-pound tin of Shirriff's orange marmalade, "No Pectin Added," which I'm sure eased the minds of anyone in the Six Towns Area who knew what pectin was.

"I suspect pectin comes from the East," Daddy said. "Most everything suspicious emanates from there."

It wasn't until the final rocket had been placed in the ground by Daddy and lighted by Bandy Wicker that anyone noticed fire was attacking the community of Doreen Beach from a number of angles.

Everyone began to run around, most getting away from the fire, but some, like Bandy Wicker and my daddy, getting closer and attempting to form some strategy for firefighting. Someone said they sure wished that Doreen Beach was located on a lake like it should be, but Doreen Beach was about four miles from Purgatory Lake and not even located on a creek, the only water coming from a communal well shared by Torval Osbaldson and the current owners of the Doreen Beach General Store, a sallow

Chinese with sunken eyes and stooped shoulders and his wispy wife who seldom came out of the attached lean-to they lived in, though they talked back and forth from the lean-to to the store, and listening to them talking was like listening to the morose gobble of turkeys.

Earl J. Rasmussen was already hauling water up from the communal well, and the sallow Chinese had donated his stock of three new galvanized water buckets, so a bucket brigade of sorts was formed, the purpose of which was to save the house of Torval and Tillie Osbaldson.

Bandy Wicker had been a volunteer firefighter in Odessa, Texas, and had brought with him to Alberta his genuine fire-fighter's hat, scoop-shaped, red and shiny, which he kept on the top shelf of the closet in his and Mrs. Bandy Wicker's bedroom. He let his son, my rabbit-snaring buddy, Floyd Wicker, try on that hat of a Christmas morning and on Floyd's birthday.

Bandy Wicker, when he lived in Odessa, Texas, had been a valued employee of the Texas Department of Highways, though even when asked directly he would avoid mentioning his capac-ity. But in large families there are no secrets. Some of the older Wicker boys were able to remember Texas, and they passed their memories on to the younger boys, who told their friends, who told their families, and soon everyone in the Six Towns Area knew that in Texas, Bandy Wicker had been armed with a half-ton truck and a shovel, assigned to patrol the highway between Odessa and El Paso, a distance of exactly 282 miles, said Daddy. Bandy Wicker's job was that of Coyote Scraper, though he also scraped armadillos, rabbits, possums, skunks, prairie dogs, and the occasional road runner who didn't under-stand the principle of two-way traffic. Daddy said Bandy Wicker preferred the title of Road Kill Disposal Engineer.

As soon as he took charge, Bandy Wicker called on his son, Floyd Wicker, to run to the Wicker homestead and fetch his genuine firefighter's hat that he had carried all the way from Odessa, Texas.

"Can't have a Fire Chief without a genuine firefighter's hat," was the way Bandy Wicker worded it.

My rabbit-snaring buddy Floyd Wicker, afraid that he'd miss something, was highly reluctant to head for the Wicker homestead, even though it was only a mile and a quarter straight down the abandoned railroad grade from Doreen Beach. Floyd wanted me to accompany him, but being afraid that I might miss something, I declined. Floyd called me a couple of unpleasant names and went on his way.

By this time the fire was making excellent progress on the bleachers behind home plate, and progress on the walls of the Doreen Beach Community Hall. The women were hauling the box lunches and trays of sandwiches and cake out of the community hall, preparing, as my mama said, for the inevitable. The fire was making some progress toward the Doreen Beach General Store, but it was built out of bricks, and the fire was approaching it from the front, so no one except the sallow Chinese and his wispy wife were worried at the moment.

The fire was also creeping with great regularity toward Slow Andy McMahon, all three hundred and some pounds of him, where he sat with his back against a cottonwood tree, sagging and shifting, in a sugar-induced coma, occasionally opening his eyes to dip another prepackaged donut from McGavin's Fine Foods into the four-pound can of Shirriff's orange marmalade, "No Pectin Added." As the fire approached his boots it was me who hollered, "Andy, move your ass or it's gonna get burnt."

Andy stared around for about thirty seconds, smiled real slow and genial before saying, "Why, Jamie O'Day, what are you doing here?"

I helped Slow Andy McMahon to his feet and led him away from the fire, which had surrounded him on three sides, me carrying the prepackaged McGavin's donuts and the four-pound tin of Shirriff's orange marmalade, "No Pectin Added."

Daddy said he guessed that one day Slow Andy McMahon, who spent his days eating his profits and sagging and settling, would just roll over and die like a barrel cactus. Daddy went on to say that when a barrel cactus got old, instead of withering and dying, it kept on growing, but it stopped growing symmetrically so it became lopsided and its own weight caused it to roll over and uproot itself.

By the time Floyd Wicker got back carrying Bandy Wicker's genuine firefighter's hat, the underpinnings of the bleachers were in flames and the back wall of the Doreen Beach Community Hall looked like it was covered in scarlet runner, and flames was licking up the front of the Doreen Beach General Store, and up the sides of the gas pump in front of the Doreen Beach General Store, and the sallow Chinese was carrying a tomato can full of water from the rear of the store and pouring it on the fire around the gas pump, though the Doreen Beach gas pump had been empty for seven years, so the prospects of an explosion were at best remote.

Gerhardt Snip, who grew potatoes and had arrived in a wagon, had a supply of gunny sacks in the wagon box. Earl J. Rasmussen poured a bucket or two of water over the gunny sacks, which produced excellent firefighting equipment. With the wet sacks, several of the men and me and my rabbit-snaring buddy Floyd Wicker whacked at the burning grass fire that was creeping up on Torval Osbaldson's house, and by the time Bandy Wicker got his genuine firefighter's hat squared away on his head and called for someone to get some wet gunny sacks and fight the fire, why, we had *saved* Torval Osbaldson's house.

In spite of having on a genuine firefighter's hat, the command to get some wet gunny sacks was the only one Bandy Wicker could come up with, consequently, the bleachers behind home plate and the Doreen Beach Community Hall fell victim to the fire, while Torval Osbaldson's house and the Doreen Beach General Store survived, which everyone interpreted as a better than 50 per cent positive result.

While the community hall was in full blaze, Sven Bjornsen and the Bjornsen Bros. Swinging Cowboy Musicmakers set up their instruments far enough away not to get toasted, and set to playing a rousing rendition of "Soldier's Joy," while those who weren't slapping out the last smouldering grass with wet gunny sacks set to dancing in the firelight. A few bottles of chokecherry wine, dandelion wine, raisin wine, home made beer, and good old heathen's rapture, bring-on-blindness, logging-boot-to-the-side-of-the-head home brew made their appearance to quench the thirst raised by the fire, and everyone danced and discussed plans for the following weekend when the bleachers and the community hall would be rebuilt.

At intermission in what was now an outdoor dance, the box lunches were auctioned off, and most of them, even Loretta Cake's, the contents of which were always highly suspect, because, Daddy said, Loretta Cake's only source of protein was her hundred-odd cats, brought, as my mama said, a pretty penny, the proceeds to go toward purchasing lumber to rebuild the bleachers and community hall.

We kids toasted sandwiches over the embers of Doreen Beach Community Hall, and dared each other to get closer to the fire than we already were. In the last second before it collapsed into a pile of burnt logs there was an instant when the community hall, fully aflame, looked exactly like the negative of a photograph.

I wondered after the winter Helen dropped by what Helen would have thought of all this. She would have been excited by the fireworks, and I bet she wouldn't have been disappointed seeing a few sickly stars dribble toward the ground. Those stars being blue, green, red, and silver would have excited Helen, and she would have giggled real pretty. I could almost hear her. I wished she lived close by so she could drop in on us regular, and we could have shared my toys and my pets. I wondered if she ever thought of me and Mama and Daddy and our big old house at the end of Nine Pin Road, and about putting a bonnet and pink dress on Abigail Uppington, and putting together a jigsaw puzzle, and reading about the three little kittens who lost their mittens, and about rat pie for supper. But I guessed Helen was probably too busy taking care of her new baby and maybe other family, and just foraging food to get by day to day, to spend much time thinking about the past.

As we were leaving for home there was a bunch of boys making fun of Lousy Louise Kortgaard, something the boys did with great regularity, and something that prompted Daddy to say on the way home, "You know, Olivia, I'm planning to do something about that girl."

SECTION TWO

Rosemary's Winter

Chapter Three

It was in the middle of winter, not the winter Helen dropped by, but an earlier winter, one that eventually became known, when all three of us were able to talk about it, as Rosemary's winter, that as I sat beside my daddy on top of a sleigh-load of freshly cut poplar, our eyes squinted against the glare of a high-skyed sun on a solid white world, that Daddy said to me, "Son, you reckon you've noticed anything unusual about your mama lately?"

The question came as a surprise; Daddy had been telling me about playing third base for a barnstorming baseball team with certain religious implications in its name, and it was easy for me to tell by his voice that playing for a barnstorming baseball team had been the happiest days of Daddy's life, and that while not exactly regretting that he could no longer play third base for a barnstorming baseball team, he wished that he had played longer or harder, or that the barnstorming baseball team had gone into bankruptcy somewhere other than Edmonton,

Alberta, so that he wouldn't now be driving across the great silence of a cold and snow-bound Alberta winter day in the aftermath of a good old freeze-the-balls-off-a-brass-monkey Alberta blizzard, but living in a warm climate, like possibly in his home state of South Carolina where, Daddy said, because of the warm weather all year round he could live forever, and he didn't mean just the length of his lifetime.

I squinted my eyes even tighter against the fierce glare of that high-skyed Alberta sun, and I ran quickly over a list of things that might be unusual or peculiar about my mama. But try as I might I couldn't think of anything, probably because I had spent almost every day of my life with her, and Mama was just there, like the big old house at the end of Nine Pin Road or the chokecherry trees full of chickadees outside the west window.

Mama had wheat-golden hair and eyes that went from corn-flower blue to bachelor button blue, about five shades darker, if she was cross with me or Daddy. She was light-skinned with just the hint of a freckle here and there, and there wasn't enough of her to fan yourself with in humid weather, Daddy said, but there certainly seemed to be a lot of her when she was cross with me or Daddy. Her voice, which was soft most of the time, could, as Daddy often said, make the tines of a pitchfork reverberate when she was angry. And when she was cross her voice could, as Daddy said, twang the cutlery.

I wondered if Mama had cut her hair and I hadn't noticed, or if she'd made herself a new dress using the old Singer treadle machine that she kept in front of the west window, so she could sew and watch the black-and-white chickadees bounce like pop-corn on the limbs of the chokecherry trees whose branches scraped and knocked deviously on the window glass whenever the wind blew, which in Alberta was most of the time.

"I can't think of anything unusual," I finally admitted, after scratching my head and racking my brains for all I was worth.

"I didn't think you had," said my daddy, scratching his mop of black curls under his tweed cap, the ear flaps down over his ears. My ear flaps were also down over my ears only I wore a leather helmet, like the one Amelia Earhart was wearing in a magazine photo my mama had pinned to the wall of her and Daddy's bedroom, just to the right of the mirror. Mama's sister, Aunt Mary Kaye, who I had never seen but once when I was too young to remember, had bought the helmet at a second-hand store in Greenville, South Carolina, for ten cents. I never determined why Mama had a photo of Amelia Earhart pinned to the wall of her and Daddy's bedroom, unless Mama had some interest in flying that she never confided to me or Daddy.

Daddy stayed silent for about a hundred yards as Barney and Babe dragged the sleigh over what in the summer was a field of red clover. When I looked at him I could see him trying to get some thoughts to his mouth so they'd come out as words in just the right order.

"Have y'all noticed that she's put on a little weight?" Daddy finally said.

I had to admit I hadn't, not that even if I had I would have considered it unusual. I shook my head.

"Well, she has," said Daddy.

"She ain't in any danger of approaching the size of Mrs. Irma Rasmussen, or the third-from-oldest Snip girl, of the Gerhardt Snips," I said by way of conversation, wondering what it was my daddy was getting at. His eyes were still all squinted up, and the words were still trying to get themselves in the proper order to exit his mouth.

Or the widow, Mrs. Beatrice Ann Stevenson, I might have added, for the widow, who was partial to Plymouth-Rock-colored dresses, had a body like an over-filled hundred-pound grain sack, with equally well-filled arms and legs. And Earl J. Rasmussen, who lived alone in the hills with about six hundred sheep, and spent a lot of his time courting the widow and letting her know that he was hers for the taking, once remarked to my daddy and to the infamous Flop Skaalrud and whoever else was behind Fark Community Hall peeing into the red willows and couch grass, that a good woman should provide heat in winter and shade in summer, which was not the way Daddy saw the world, as there was scarcely enough of Mama to fan yourself with in humid weather, unless there had been a drastic change in her that I had completely failed to detect, which there must have been or Daddy wouldn't have been quizzing me.

"Son," he said, "do you understand about where babies come from?"

"Yes," I said quickly. Then, "No," just as quickly. Then, after pausing for a few seconds to get my thoughts together so they'd come out of my mouth as words in the right order, I said, "Yes, I believe I do."

"Well, that is what I'm getting at, son. Your mama and I didn't say anything because we thought you'd notice, but I guess you being around her every day, and the changes being so gradual and all . . . anyway, we figure about the time the snow melts and Jamie O'Day Creek floods, why you'll have yourself a baby brother or sister."

I just squinted up my eyes against the high-skyed blue glare of the cold Alberta winter in the aftermath of a good old freeze-the-balls-off-a-brass-monkey Alberta blizzard, while I tried to digest what Daddy had just told me.

I was the only kid in the Six Towns Area, except my sometime-playmate, Velvet Rasmussen Bozniak, who didn't have a whole passel of brothers and sisters, and Velvet Rasmussen Bozniak didn't have brothers or sisters because her daddy, Arthur Bozniak, a full-scholarshipped orphaned genius, had been killed in World War Two, or if that wasn't exactly the whole truth it was the simplest way to explain Velvet's situation, which was good enough for everyone in the Six Towns Area, when they weren't being catty, which, Mama said, was most of the time.

My rabbit-snaring buddy Floyd Wicker had six older brothers who protected him from outsiders, but regularly pounded him out, sometimes just for getting on their nerves. Floyd had one younger sister, a five-year-old named Gretchen, who everybody, including Floyd, protected and spoiled. I thought about Gretchen Wicker's orangish ringlets, and how she smiled like she was looking over the rims of glasses, though she didn't wear glasses, and how Floyd and all the Wicker boys would pound anyone who said anything even halfway bad about their baby sister, let alone anyone who touched her, and I decided that it would be more than tolerable to have someone to protect.

"I reckon I'd like a sister," I said to my daddy.

"Your mama and I are partial to a girl this time," Daddy said. "We thought we might call her Rosemary," Daddy went on, "though we won't be disappointed if it's a boy, and if it was we'd call him Gene Stratton Porter O'Day."

I said Rosemary sounded fine to me, but if it was a boy, I was more partial to Jack London O'Day, because *The Call of the Wild* was about my most favorite book.

"He didn't bat an eye," Daddy said to Mama, late that evening when they thought I was sleeping. "He'd prefer a girl, but he didn't ask any questions, and he didn't seem much surprised or very excited. I guess it's hard to shock kids nowadays."

The reason I didn't ask any questions was I couldn't think of any, and the reason I didn't seem very surprised or excited was because I was so surprised, not so much at Mama having a baby, but at what Mama and Daddy must have had to do in order to accomplish a baby.

Mama and Daddy conspiring to have a baby proved me wrong. And being proved wrong by a girl, a smart aleck girl at that, was something I didn't take kindly to. When Daddy was telling me that I was going to have a baby brother or sister about the time the snow melted and Jamie O'Day Creek flooded, I was thinking that I had been proved wrong by a smart aleck girl, Velvet Rasmussen Bozniak.

I was thinking I must be a lot stupider than I ever supposed for Mama to get two-thirds of a baby built without me noticing. I was determined that for the rest of my life I would be able to spot a pregnant woman from at least across a room, and maybe even farther away than that. I checked things out immediately we got back to our big old house at the end of Nine Pin Road, and though there still was barely enough of Mama to fan yourself with on a humid day, which surely must have been a South Carolina expression, for in Alberta there were no humid days, Mama had become considerably wider across the hips, and her belly resembled the belly of Adolf Snip, who was short and rotund and wore wide suspenders to hold up his black work pants; and Mama resembled every woman in the Six Towns Area who I had seen while they were expecting a baby.

Most of all I was thinking about having to confess to Velvet Rasmussen Bozniak that I was going to have a brother or sister, which meant my mama and daddy actually did what Velvet Rasmussen Bozniak said they did in order to build a baby, something I had denied to her and to myself, every time Velvet Rasmussen Bozniak brought the subject up, which was every time Velvet Rasmussen Bozniak and I were alone, which was far too often for my comfort.

Though we were the same age, Velvet Rasumussen Bozniak seemed to know more about almost every subject than I did, especially about what people did in order to build a baby, and on more than one occasion when we were alone Velvet Rasmussen Bozniak offered to give me a practical demonstration, an opportunity I would decline, not too graciously, saving myself by dangling Velvet Rasmussen Bozniak's Shirley Temple doll over the firebox of the cook stove.

When she saw her Shirley Temple doll dangling over the firebox of the cook stove, Velvet Rasmussen Bozniak would scream bloody murder and forget all about providing a demonstration of baby-building, and her mother, Mrs. Edytha Rasmussen Bozniak, would look up from the cup of tea she was drinking at the oilcloth-covered kitchen table and say, "Now you children play nicely."

Chapter Four

"Your daddy," Mama often remarked, "bless his heart, has a lot of interesting ideas, and it's not always his fault that they don't pan out." Here she paused, staring out the east window of our big old house at the end of Nine Pin Road, where we could see the remnants of wooden fences sinking into the earth. "Sometimes there is considerable fault on your daddy's part. Other times he just does not follow through on his ideas the way a normal person would."

Keeping Mama's remarks in mind, I decided that when I built the cradle for my brother or sister, I was not going to get in trouble the way Daddy did, through no fault of his own, or through considerable fault of his own, but was going to follow through on my idea the way a normal person would.

As an example of what Mama meant about Daddy having interesting ideas, and about them not always panning out, was something that happened before I was born, in the first year that Mama and Daddy lived on the farm at the end of Nine Pin Road.

Daddy discovered early on that his quarter-section was not good for raising grain and would produce nothing except a little red clover and timothy hay, neither of which were a decent cash crop. The land, Daddy said, was conducive to grazing, so when he heard a rumor that a livestock dealer in Edmonton, Weiller and Williams Stockyards, would loan out scrawny animals they had bought in the spring to be fattened up over the summer, and in the fall pay so much a pound for the weight the animals gained, Daddy thought that the situation was tailor-made to his aspirations for a cash crop and his stony and worthless land.

Cattle, Daddy said, could graze on the lush wild hay, and tame timothy hay, and maybe even on some of the red clover in the north pasture, and they could water at Jamie O'Day Creek, and at several small sloughs scattered about like bluish eyes in the hollows of the hopeless quarter-section.

By the time Daddy arranged a ride to Edmonton in the cab of Curly's inherited dump truck, which smelled strongly of grease and oil, carbon monoxide, cigarette smoke, and Curly McClintock, and by the time Daddy stopped off at Weiller and Williams Stockyards to discuss the rumor he had heard, all the scrawny cattle had been assigned to other farmers. What grazing animals left to choose from were scrawny sheep and scrawny pigs.

Daddy said there was something unmanly about sheep, though he never made that statement in front of his friend Earl J. Rasmussen, who lived back in the hills with about six hundred sheep, and spent his spare time courting the widow, Mrs. Beatrice Ann Stevenson, when he wasn't reciting *Casey at the Bat* at box socials, sports days, community dances, and ethnic weddings, so Daddy decided on pigs, which, Mama said, was his first mistake, because whereas cattle and sheep could be kept nearby, enclosed by the barbed-wire fences that already surrounded our pitiful quarter-section of land, pigs required special pens with wooden slats flush with the ground, because a pig's favorite, and apparently only, interest other than filling its stomach was to tunnel to freedom under the wooden fences.

Daddy soon found out that scrawny pigs could live passably well off the land, eating tall stands of pig weed, which I suppose was named because pigs liked to eat it, and dig up wild parsnips and other roots, but that the land had to be changed frequently, which meant that Daddy, instead of relaxing on the front porch of our big old house at the end of Nine Pin Road and watching a herd of scrawny cattle or a flock of scrawny sheep fattening up in front of his very eyes on the otherwise useless land, found himself spending most of his waking hours rearranging the maze of fences so as to give the pigs new land to root and graze, and patrolling the perimeter of those fences, whacking large stupid pink snouts with a hoe handle, as they attempted to tunnel their way to freedom.

By the end of the summer the pigs, Daddy said, were fat and sleek as if they'd been blown up by an air hose, and when the trucks from Weiller and Williams Stockyards arrived, the drivers remarked on the quality of the hogs, and how they would bring the finest price.

Unfortunately, in order to build the maze of fences, Daddy had had to borrow money from the Imperial Bank at Sangudo. Daddy had arrived in the Six Towns Area too late to borrow from Banker Olaf Gordonjensen and the Bank of New Oslo, which had failed in 1929, like most banks in North America.

Daddy built the maze of fences and instead of relaxing on the front porch that summer watching a herd of cattle, or a flock of sheep grow fat off the land, Daddy spent most of his summer moving that maze of fences about, a section at a time, so the pigs could have fresh land to root, fresh pig weed to eat and fresh wild parsnips to discover.

After the pigs were returned and the money came in from Weiller and Williams Stockyards, the Imperial Bank in Sangudo had to be paid. Unfortunately, as the pigs fattened, the price of hogs had dwindled, so a deal that looked profitable in April did not look that way in September, when, on the Tuesday after Labor Day, the trucks from Weiller and Williams Stockyards arrived to cart the hogs off to their well-deserved fate.

Daddy said he wished he could travel along and watch every one of those pigs trussed up by the ankle and sent along a conveyor line to have its stupid pink throat slit, for by the end of the summer, Daddy hated the fence, and Daddy hated the hogs with their big, stupid pink snouts always poking out from under the fence like humungous worms. The loan to the Imperial Bank in Sangudo and the small feed bill came to within a dollar or two of the amount Daddy received from Weiller and Williams Stockyards for boarding the pigs all summer, not leaving him any income for moving the sections of fence, and for patrolling the perimeter, and whacking large stupid pink snouts with a hoe handle as they tried to tunnel to freedom.

All Daddy had to show for his summer of labor was a maze of wooden fences, which he vowed he would never use again because of the hatred of pigs he had acquired over the summer.

"You didn't make a penny for a whole summer's work," Mama pointed out unnecessarily, her voice twanging with irritation, her blue eyes several shades darker than they usually were, a lot closer to bachelor-button than cornflower blue.

"Well, look at it this way, Olivia," my daddy said, scratching his mop of black curls and shuffling papers on the oilcloth-covered kitchen table, papers that no matter how he shuffled them showed that all he had to show for his summer's work was a maze of wooden fences he vowed never to use again, "we had the use of the pigs."

For the rest of her life Mama loved to tell that story of what was most lovable about my daddy and what was most frustrating about my daddy.

Chapter Five

My decision to build a cradle for my forthcoming brother or sister was based on a couple of considerations, one being that since my daddy, in better times, had built fine houses in Edmonton and elsewhere, that I had perhaps inherited some of my daddy's talent for building things, and the other being my determination to follow through on my project as a normal person would.

I quickly discovered that I had not inherited any of my Daddy's talent for building, and when, not too long after I started, Daddy tried to intervene in the project, I discovered that there are a number of types of carpentry involved in building fine houses, and the type of carpentry that my daddy specialized in was everything except finely detailed work, which I discovered was what building a cradle, especially contriving and completing a design for the headboard and footboard, was defined as.

I had taken the two ends of a wooden apple box and attacked them with sandpaper and several long, thin files, a thick rasp, a plane, a hammer and chisel, a fret saw, and a hand saw. My plan involved turning the two more-or-less square pieces of wood into a headboard and a footboard for the cradle. Unfortunately, the people who make apple boxes use very hard wood for the ends, and, also unfortunately, the only place warm enough to work during an Alberta winter was the kitchen. For Mama's benefit, I had to lie concerning what it was that I was building. A toy box for myself, I believe I said.

After several days of sandpapering I managed to get most of the paper label advertising Trustworthy Apples of Yakima, Washington, sandpapered off each end of the apple box. But it didn't seem to matter how much I filed or rasped, hammered and chiseled, or worked with a fret saw, hand saw, or plane, the two more or less square pieces of hardwood remained two more or less square pieces of hardwood.

It was about the fourth day when it appeared that in spite of my good intentions, I was, like my daddy, not going to be able to follow through on the project as a normal person would, that Daddy decided to help me out. Daddy chipped away with the hammer and chisel, sawed with the fret saw, sawed even harder with the hand saw, smoothed with the plane, and rasped with the rasp. Unfortunately, the two more or less square pieces of hardwood remained relatively unchanged. At that point Daddy decided to round the corners of the two more or less square pieces of hardwood by chipping at them with his big, blue, double-bitted ax that he used to split firewood.

The two more or less square pieces of hardwood did not react positively to being attacked with Daddy's big, blue, double-bitted ax, and cracked, one into two pieces, the other into three, making them useless as prospective headboards and footboards.

After I was supposed to be asleep that night, Mama chastised Daddy for his carelessness, not fully realizing, when it came to carpentry, what Daddy was good at and what Daddy was not good at, and Daddy simply listened to Mama twang the cutlery.

The next morning Daddy suggested that he harness up our team of blacks, Barney and Babe, to the sleigh, and that I accompany him on a nine-mile drive toward Magnolia, where there was rumored to be a fellow known as Oslin the Estonian, who was a furniture maker.

Oslin the Estonian was a tall, stoop-shouldered man with a long, sad face the shape of an anvil. He had thin wrists but the hands that dangled below were huge. Oslin the Estonian lived in an unpainted, slant-roofed shack that housed a wife and an indeterminate number of children. The only outbuildings were a tumbledown log barn and a granary, and it was in the granary, heated by a smudge fire, green wood and sod smoldering in a battered pail, that Oslin did his carpenter work. Even in the cold of the winter, the smell of fresh cut wood and linseed oil overpowered the thick odor of the smudge. Oslin was just finishing a spinning wheel, the wood, my daddy said later, as pale as a Southern belle. Oslin was also at work on a high-chair, a variety of wooden churns, some small, some large, and a small cabinet on which he had carved a row of roses as real as the ones Mama grew on the south side of our house. Oslin the Estonian smiled, gestured, and it wasn't until some time later I realized that Oslin was unable to speak.

If Daddy and Oslin the Estonian had joined forces they could have been carpenters to the world. Oslin did only detail work, Daddy did only rough work, but both were masters at their specialties.

Eventually, Oslin, by hooking his arm in the shape of a scythe and gesturing as if he were cutting weeds, invited us into the tiny house, where I found myself enveloped by a number of small Oslins.

The shack was only about fifteen feet in each direction, a tiny kitchen and two bedrooms, partitioned by walls shoulder high.

All the children (at first I thought there were four, then five, then six) slept in one bed, and it was there that I was enveloped by Oslins, in the stale but friendly confines of a dozen home-made quilts and down comforters.

"Papa can't talk," one of the enveloping Oslins, a girl with the same long, anvil-shaped face as her father, said, giggling and hiding her face in a well-worn satin comforter.

It had occurred vaguely to me that Oslin hadn't spoken, but I had assumed it was because he didn't speak English, something not uncommon in the Six Towns Area.

"What language does he speak?" I asked.

"He don't," said a voice from the end of the bed, a seventh little Oslin, a boy with crooked teeth and his father's anvil-shaped face.

"He was borned that way," said another, a girl with a round, sunny face that resembled her mother's.

A boy about my age liked to wrestle and soon we were tumbling like otters among the sheets, quilts, blankets, comforters, and pillows.

"Watch out for the baby," one of the girls yelled as the Oslin boy who liked to wrestle catapulted me off the bed. I instinctively changed the direction of my fall, and missed an apple-box crib by a few inches. Inside the apple-box crib, wrapped in a pink blanket and wearing a pink bonnet was the newest Oslin, a girl called something close to Oxanna, the ninth and newest Oslin.

Having no brothers or sisters and no close neighbors with children, I was both backward and awkward about playing with other children, although ravenous for their company. I tried to imagine what it would be like if I were, say, the fourth or fifth, or eighth, or ninth, and if our family were known to outsiders as the enveloping O'Days.

I had trouble imagining that, for the only thing I ever wrestled with was my cowardly dog, Benito Mussolini, who had whiskers that stuck out like a cat's and bad breath, and who was afraid of cats, prairie dogs, blue jays, cattle, pigs, horses, water, the dark, and probably inanimate objects as well.

I stared at Oxanna, the ninth and newest enveloping Oslin, as she waved her tiny hands in front of her doll-sized pink face. The girl who had warned me about falling on the baby named, I think, Katarinka, picked the baby up, roughly I thought, though the baby only gurgled and smiled.

"You can hold her," Katarinka said.

I declined, afraid that I'd hurt her, but I held my hand out and Oxanna, the newest enveloping Oslin, seized my little finger with her whole hand and hung on with a surprising tenacity.

Katarinka was kissing Oxanna frequently, on both cheeks, on her little flat baby nose, on her forehead and little ears.

"You can kiss her, if you want," Katarinka said, and I did. I kissed her little flat baby nose a couple of times, as the smallest Oslin gurgled and smiled, and I decided that having a baby sister, or even a brother, wouldn't be bad at all.

Somehow Daddy and Oslin the Estonian agreed that Oslin would build a crib from white birch and that it would be ready in two weeks.

I didn't think about it until we were on our way home, but it was odd that Oxanna was asleep in an apple-box crib, almost identical to the one Daddy and I tried to make except Oxanna's crib still had the paper labels on each end, advertising Tom Cat Apples of Oliver, British Columbia. I mentioned to Daddy that it seemed odd for a man like Oslin the Estonian, who built beautiful furniture for others, to have his own daughter sleeping in an apple box. I had noticed also, that the Oslins didn't seem to own a spinning wheel, or a wooden butter churn, although I didn't get to their barn to check to see if they had beautifully made milk stools.

"Tradesmen," Daddy said, "seldom make use of their own

skills around their own home." I was skeptical at the time, but I
have come to see, in time, that it is true.

Mama was due to produce my brother or sister around the final
week of April, just about the time that the last snow melted and
Jamie O'Day Creek flooded everything in view with a thin rip-
pling coat of water that looked stained and brownish, the color
influenced by the brown grasses from the previous fall.

In only a few weeks, Jamie O'Day Creek would recede within
its banks; by mid-summer it would be no thicker than a broom
handle, and by fall it would disappear altogether. When the leaves
fell, where the banks of Jamie O'Day Creek had been would be
all brown crinkly leaves, the transient nature of the creek being,
my daddy said, why Jamie O'Day Creek was not on any map,
and why it was known as Jamie O'Day Creek only to us.

Mama, except for having lived in Colombia for a while,
where her daddy was an engineer for an emerald mine, was used
to more civilized circumstances than were available in Fark and
vicinity. As a result, Mama insisted that she was entitled to have
her baby in the exact same place, the University Hospital at the
far south end of the High Level Bridge, in Edmonton, where I
had been born. And, on the rare occasions when Mama felt
entitled to something, Daddy, one way or another, usually saw
to it that she got her way. So Daddy arranged for Mama, when
her time came, to go to the University Hospital at the far end of
the High Level Bridge in Edmonton, in spite of the fact that
Loretta Cake, who fancied herself a midwife, made at least two
calls on Mama as soon as the word got out that Mama was
expecting. Loretta Cake arrived at our house at the end of Nine
Pin Road dressed in long skirts, bangles, and head scarves, leading her eight square-jawed tom cats on leashes.

"Y'all carrying a crystal ball with you?" Daddy asked, meaning it as a joke, but Loretta Cake took some time to explain in

her odd accent, which may or may not have been English, that she could make prognostications by the growth of moss on the north side of trees, by whether scarlet runner twined to the right or the left, and, if all else failed, by studying dog entrails, and because of that she did not need to go to the expense of acquiring a crystal ball. Loretta Cake made her statement about dog entrails while staring at my cowardly dog Benito Mussolini so directly that Benito Mussolini whined and slunk as far back behind the cook stove as he could get.

Mama thanked Loretta Cake for her trouble, at the same time declining to spit on a flat, bluish rock that Loretta Cake drew from one of her many pockets, so that Loretta could read her fortune in the spittle.

Getting Mama to the University Hospital, at the far south end of the High Level Bridge in Edmonton, was all a matter of timing, Daddy claimed and Mama more or less agreed. Since Mama didn't really know anyone in Edmonton that she could stay with or, more likely, was too proud to be beholden, it was important that she not go to Edmonton too soon, and, the roads being impassible and pretty well non-existent in April in the Six Towns Area, it was important that she not set out too late.

I was both looking forward to and dreading the time Mama would be gone. I had never been away from Mama for more than a long day and a couple of occasions overnight when she traveled with Curly McClintock to Edmonton to shop and, I guess, visit the doctor when I hadn't yet comprehended she was pregnant.

On a day when I could stand at the east window and watch the snowbanks, under a brilliant sun, grow soft and inch toward the earth, a day about two weeks before Mama went off to the University Hospital at the far south end of the High Level Bridge in Edmonton, Alberta, Rosemary O'Day or Gene Stratton Porter O'Day kicked my hand through Mama's belly.

"You should feel this," Mama said. Mama had on a frilly blue bib-apron that went around her neck, with ties around her waist. She was stirring something at the cook stove, while I finished my breakfast at the oilcloth-covered kitchen table.

"Feel what?" I said, crunching toast.

"Feel this baby kick," Mama said.

Until that time, it had not occurred to me that the would-be brother or sister was alive before it was actually born. Daddy had got out the battered encyclopedia with the one volume missing, Daddy and Mama having different explanations for how the one volume got to be missing, and read a couple of pages to me about the human reproductive system, and he showed me diagrams that looked like a tiny baby curled up inside a concrete silo, but I didn't really pay a lot of attention, and Daddy, feeling he had done his duty, didn't press the matter.

"Come here," Mama said. And when I wasn't quick about it she added, "This thing ain't gonna hurt you."

I sidled over to the cook stove, but when Mama turned around and faced me I had to take a step backwards to escape the bulk of her.

I put my hand very tentatively on the front of the frilly blue apron.

"Heaven's sake," said Mama. "Don't have to be so gentle. Thing ain't about to bite you. Babies are tougher than you might imagine."

She took my hand and placed it firmly on her belly. I had sat on Mama's knee for goodness knows how many hundred hours and had touched Mama without ever thinking about it, but standing in front of her and my would-be brother or sister, I felt embarrassed.

"Ain't nothing to be afraid of," Mama said.

She held my hand there on her taut belly and sure enough, the baby, my would-be brother or sister, Rosemary O'Day or

Gene Stratton Porter O'Day, kicked my hand, not just once, but two, three, four times in a row.

"Baby's getting more than a mite sprightly," Mama said, smiling down at me.

Chapter Six

A year or two before Daddy had to point out to me that there had been changes in Mama that I should have noticed if I had been even passingly observant, Daddy had delivered to me his lecture on sex education. He'd taken me to Edmonton to do it, as Daddy was not one for talking about sex education where anyone he might know could listen in. There were business considerations that took Daddy to Edmonton, but it was with the idea of delivering me a lecture on sex education that Daddy invited me to go along, only the second time in my life, since I could remember, that I had visited Edmonton.

On the other occasion, when I had accompanied Mama on the eastbound Western Trailways bus, I didn't enjoy myself a whole lot. In fact, I threw up inside the westbound Western Trailways bus on the return trip, so I thought I would compare visiting the city with Daddy as opposed to Mama.

To begin with, Daddy and me didn't catch the eastbound Western Trailways bus at Bjornsen's Corner; we arranged a ride with Curly McClintock in the cab of his inherited dump truck. We had to get up at 4:00 A.M. while a pale moon was still shining on the fields and roads, and Daddy hitched our old roan horse, Ethan Allen, to the buggy and we drove the more or less five miles to the old Fark station house that the McClintocks took over as their homestead about thirty minutes after the railroad abandoned it.

Daddy unhooked Ethan Allen and tethered him in a meadow, while Mrs. Edina McClintock, Curly's mama, mother-in-law to Gunhilda Gordonjensen McClintock and widow of Black Darren McClintock, who about fifteen years before had pushed back from the table after a feed of partridge parts and fried turnips, unbuckled his belt, and passed away, a woman who, Daddy said, never slept as far as he could tell, prepared us each a cup of hot tea with a lot of sugar and lemon in it.

The sun was peeking up like rose petals when Curly McClintock's truck came rumbling down what used to be the railroad grade, and pulled up in front of what had once been the Fark station house.

Daddy and me climbed up in the cab, which smelled of grease, oil, carbon monoxide, sour milk, cigarette smoke, and Curly McClintock, taking our cups of tea with us, and Mrs. Edina McClintock handed him only a cup of hot tea with plenty of sugar and lemon in it, and the dump truck grumbled off down what used to be the railroad grade in the direction of the Edmonton–Jasper Highway.

Curly McClintock let us off at the Edmonton City Dairy on 109th Street, one of the places Curly dropped off cream cans full of cream. The Edmonton City Dairy, Daddy pointed out, was one of the landmarks of Edmonton, for a hundred-foot-high white plaster milk bottle marked its location.

Soon as we were out of the truck we stood and gawked for a while at the hundred-foot-high white plaster milk bottle until

Daddy led the way to Jasper Avenue, where we waited for a streetcar in front of an auto dealership that would have sold new Studebaker cars if there had been any to sell that year, but there weren't because there was a war on, so the auto dealership only had used Studebakers, Chevrolets, Fords, Terraplanes, Hudsons, Nashes, and DeSotos on their lot.

The streetcar ride with Daddy was something I enjoyed. The time I traveled to Edmonton with Mama, she said, "Well, it's early and we're both healthy. We can walk downtown. We may wish we had the streetcar money later in the day."

Daddy had an appointment with a lawyer, something to do with the mortgage on the farm, I gathered. The lawyer's office was on the top floor of the McLeod Building, at eight stories the tallest building in all Edmonton and, Daddy said, very possibly the tallest structure between Vancouver and Toronto. We rode to the very top floor, and I hung on to Daddy's hand as the bottom dropped out of my stomach when the elevator took off.

In the reception room, I looked out across Edmonton, and people below us looked like ants and buildings looked like doll-buildings, and Daddy said it was as near to heaven as him or me was ever likely to get.

"If that fellow stood next to one of our unpainted granaries you wouldn't be able to see him," Daddy whispered as the lawyer advanced across the waiting room.

The lawyer made a big fuss over me, but it was all phony. He brought out a crumpled paper bag and offered me horrible brown candy that I took out of my mouth as soon as he turned his back. Daddy said later it was horehound, and I could believe it because it tasted like my cowardly dog Benito Mussolini had peed on it.

Once, while Daddy was gone down the hall, I thought I heard my Daddy's voiced raised like when he was calling out the

Catholic Church or the Government, or the Eastern financiers who kept the West poor.

"It's easier to talk to a stone," Daddy said, while we waited for the elevator back down to earth, "and a stone has a darn sight more common sense."

I soon discovered that it was much more exciting to be in Edmonton with Daddy than it had been being there with Mama. Mama's approach was to get everything done and then see if there was time and money, particularly money, left to buy or do anything else.

Daddy's approach was to do things at random and hope there would be some time and money left at the end of the day. Consequently, right after we left the tallest building in Edmonton, and maybe the tallest building between Vancouver and Toronto, we walked around a corner and crossed a street or two and were confronted by about a million flashing lightbulbs that spelled out "Rialto Theatre."

After I asked, Daddy said he didn't know what *Rialto* meant, if it meant anything, and that in Canada they didn't know how to spell *theater* or *center*, and always reversed the last two letters, even though they pronounced them the same as real Americans, and didn't pronounce them the-at-ree, or cent-ree.

After we studied the posters, we determined that the first show was about to begin, and that it was a color movie about Buffalo Bill Cody.

Daddy counted the money he had in the inside pocket of his overalls, and said he reckoned the movie would be an educational experience for me, and didn't I reckon it would be an educational experience? I said that I reckoned a movie about Buffalo Bill Cody would be a very educational experience, and at that moment I really enjoyed being with Daddy, because when I'd come to Edmonton with Mama she had also counted the money, which was pinned in a change purse inside her black leather handbag, and said she reckoned we couldn't afford the luxury of attending a movie, mainly because I needed some new britches and new shoes, both of which I would gladly have given up in order to see a color movie about Buffalo Bill Cody, though the movie Mama almost took me to was called *Naughty Marietta* and was about a lot of ladies in hoop skirts who stood around the gardens and sang a lot, and the posters were in black and white.

Daddy paid our way into the theater and bought us a bag of pink popcorn and a string of red licorice each — Mama might have sprung for popcorn for me, but she wouldn't have got anything for herself, which would have made me feel guilty, and she wouldn't have shared the popcorn when I offered, which I would have — and we went in and sat on plush red-velvet seats where we sunk right down out of sight.

The first thing to come on was a newsreel in black and white with an announcer who had a voice-of-doom tone, just like Lorne Greene who delivered the CBC News every evening on the radio and rattled the dinner plates and made small children cry. But then came a Tom and Jerry cartoon, and it was like the Sunday funnies in the *Star Weekly* come to life, and I grabbed Daddy's sleeve and said "Look at that!"

And Daddy, who had a laugh that was really a guffaw and could never be mistaken for anything else, guffawed when a cat fell face-first into a vat of cement, and Daddy slapped his thigh, and said "Jamie, son, you ain't seen nothin' yet," and he guffawed again.

A woman about two rows in front of us, there weren't more than twenty people in the theater, turned around and bugged her eyes at us and said "Do you mind?"

"Heck, no, Ma'am," Daddy said, "we don't mind. That little bitty hat you're wearin' don't block our view at all. It don't block yours does it, Jamie? You just go on and enjoy yourself,

Ma'am. This here's my son, Jamie. It's the first time he's been to a moving picture show."

The woman sniffed mightily and turned back around to face the screen, sliding down on her neck as she did so.

We were riding the streetcar from downtown all the way to Calder, near the Canadian National Railway yards, Daddy said, to Mrs. Oppenheim's house, a woman Daddy always referred to, except to her face, as Oppie. The winter Helen dropped by, when we had the pig living in our kitchen, my daddy wanted to name that pig Oppie, after Mama's friend's sister, Mrs. Oppenheim, but Mama wouldn't let him.

"Little pitchers have big ears," she said, and went on to ask what if Jamie was to repeat the name of our pig to someone who knew Mrs. Oppenheim or knew Mrs. Oppenheim's sister? And Daddy finally agreed, against his better judgment, he said, to call the pig Abigail Uppington, after the character on the radio who came to visit Fibber McGee every week, and acted high and mighty when she did so.

Daddy said there was a Mr. Oppenheim, such as he was, but since we were arriving late and leaving early, we might manage to miss him, as he worked the graveyard shift at the Calder Yards, if you could call sleeping in a grease pit, wrapped in a nice home-made quilt, work.

Mr. Oppenheim, Daddy said, had slipped through the cracks of the railroad bureaucracy several years before: the railroad stopped giving him work assignments but continued to send his pay check every two weeks. Mr. Oppenheim reported to work every night as always, but curled up in an unused grease pit and slept his shift away. A year or two after he slipped through the cracks, Mr. Oppenheim applied for a day job as a railroad car cleaner and got it, so he got up from his sleep and reported to work as a railroad car cleaner. Then Mr. Oppenheim went home and ate supper and spent the evening with Mrs. Oppenheim until it was time for him to take his home-made quilt and head for the railroad yards to sleep the night away in an abandoned grease pit to collect his second set of wages. Mrs. Oppenheim said she missed Mr. Oppenheim, having him away all night, but, she added, she hadn't been pregnant since 1929, when Mr. Oppenheim began sleeping in the grease pit at Calder Railroad Yards, and she suspected one event had some connection with the other.

It was while we were on the way to Mrs. Oppenheim's, riding at the very back of the streetcar on the wide wicker seat, the only passengers, that Daddy gave me his lecture on sex education.

It had been a long day. Mama had tugged me out of bed before 4:00 A.M., and we had traveled five miles by horse and buggy, then to Edmonton in Curly McClintock's inherited dump truck, visited the lawyer, visited the doctor to get my ears looked at because both Daddy and Mama felt I might have a hearing problem since I tended to have to be spoken to several times before I gave any indication of hearing — the doctor shone a flashlight in my ears and rang a tuning fork in various parts of the room, then said my hearing was 100 per cent, and the reason I tended not to answer inquiries was probably that I was an inveterate day dreamer, which has turned out to be true. We had seen two moving picture shows, one of them about Buffalo Bill Cody, eaten lunch at the Belmont Café, and eaten dinner at the King Edward Hotel Café, which was about a thousand miles distant from the Belmont Café in quality, and, as Daddy said, ambience.

Daddy began his lecture on sex education by saying, "Jamie, son, I need to have a little talk with you." And Daddy, who was never known to take the short way when the long way would do, went into a discourse on the mating habits of animals and birds, something I was not particularly interested in. He even said that if we had a female dog within six miles of Nine Pin

Road, why, we might have puppies, but then said that he doubted my cowardly dog Benito Mussolini would know what to do with a female dog even if he run smack up against one.

Eventually, Daddy got to talking about when two human beings, a man and a woman, run smack up against each other, them having reproduction on their minds.

Well, Daddy said "reproduction," and Daddy said "intercourse," and Daddy said "organ," and Daddy said "love," and Daddy said "respect," and then Daddy said another word very quietly but not so quietly I couldn't hear it, and he said it was a word I was never ever to repeat, even though I would occasionally hear the men use it, usually when they were out in the corral or behind Fark Community Hall peeing in the red willow clumps and bunch grass, and I would be sure to hear boys my age and older use it if and when I ever got to attend a proper school.

I promised that I would never use the word, which I had no recollection of hearing, and when Daddy eventually wound down and asked if I had any questions, I shook my head, being really glad that the lecture on sex education was over. It was very warm in the streetcar, the conductor had a coal stove, a little black coal scuttle, a little black coal shovel, and he had stoked the stove before we set off from downtown Edmonton. I was more asleep than awake when Daddy finally finished his lecture on sex education.

To top off the lecture, Daddy pulled from the pocket of his overalls a Wildfire chocolate bar, the kind with the purple wrapper with red and yellow flames licking down the middle of it. I perked up at the sight of the Wildfire chocolate bar, and managed to get it all eaten by the time we got to Mrs. Oppenheim's, getting hardly any on me, Daddy said, as he wiped my face with his big, red-checkered handkerchief under the streetlight outside the Oppenheims' house.

I thought a little about Daddy's lecture on sex education as I was drifting off to sleep in a bed with crisp white sheets, but it only took me a few seconds to get to sleep, and in the morning I couldn't for the life of me remember the word Daddy told me never ever to say, even if I heard it, which I couldn't recall ever having done. And I certainly didn't have the nerve to ask Daddy what the word was, because then he'd know that I hadn't been interested in what he'd told me, and he had brought me to Edmonton with the express purpose of delivering his sex education lecture, and I didn't want Daddy to be disappointed in me.

What I did remember, and word for word, was something Daddy told me over dinner at the King Edward Hotel Café, something that I was interested in, and something that I had never in my life suspected, and something that it must have taken Daddy a lot of courage to tell me.

We were sitting in the King Edward Hotel Café, which, Daddy said, if it wasn't the best restaurant in Edmonton, was certainly close enough that no one would argue. Daddy was finishing a T-bone steak with french-fried potatoes and onion rings, and I was eating fat little pork sausages in a spicy tomato gravy and planning on lemon pie for dessert, when Daddy leaned across the white linen tablecloth which felt thick as canvas, and said, "You know Jamie, son, how proud I am of the way you've learned to read and write, how you just seemed to teach yourself to do both."

I didn't say anything. I was waiting to see what Daddy was leading up to.

"You know, son, how you've met your Mama's family — her sister and your grandparents?"

I nodded, chewing my sausage. I had a vague recollection of my grandparents, though I didn't think I'd recognize either of them if I met them on the road. And Mama's sister, my Aunt Mary Kaye, who lived in Greenville, South Carolina, had visited once when I was too young to remember.

"You also know you haven't met any of my family," Daddy went on. "I do have family; you have another set of grandparents in South Carolina — well, your grandaddy's gone to his reward, but you do have a grandmother and three aunties. I don't know if you know the difference, Jamie, but there's poor, and there's sorrowful, and there's shiftless, and unfortunately my family falls in the latter two categories.

"As both me and your Mama have said many a time, there's no crime in being poor, that's something forced on people by powers they can't control, but people choose to be sorrowful and choose to be shiftless, and that was what my family chose.

"I've never spent a single day of my life in school, and that is something I'm certainly not proud of, and it's why I see that you study your lessons by mail even though we are too far from a school for you to attend regular."

"But you read and write," I said.

"I do, because of your mama. My family were so sorrowful and so shiftless that they didn't send a one of us kids to school without having the law on their tail. By the time the girls came along schooling was the law, so they each got a few years, enough to read and write. But not me. I couldn't see no reason why I should read and write.

"It didn't take no reading or writing ability to be a sharecroppers' son, and it didn't take no reading or writing ability to be in the army and get gassed in World War One, and it didn't take no reading or writing ability to play minor league baseball, and it didn't take no reading or writing ability to be a gandy dancer for the railroad.

"What I discovered was that all the things I could do without knowing how to read and write didn't take any talent. My own daddy couldn't read or write, and I don't suppose Mama could either.

"It's an odd feeling, Jamie, son, not being able to read and write in a world where most everyone can. It was like having a leg or an arm missing, only people feel some sympathy for folks who have a leg or arm missing, but not for a fellow who can't read or write, so that fellow, he hides what's missing, and gets downright sneaky and conniving in order to keep his secret. It just gnaws away at you, son, like TB or one of them wasting diseases that kills from the inside out.

"There is a whole world out there that functions with the written word, a whole world that I didn't even know about. Like books. We both take books for granted now. I read books to you, and I read the complete novel in the *Toronto Star Weekly* every week.

"I had chances, especially in the army, to learn to read and write. There was a doctor I worked with in the medical corps, took a liking to me, he did. Said I had the talent and disposition to be a doctor, and said he'd give me the best recommendation in the world if I wanted to go to medical school when I got out of the army. But I just sort of smiled and said I didn't reckon I could afford to go to medical school. Seemed to me if I told him I couldn't read I was admitting I was dumb, and nobody ever wants to admit that they're dumb.

"What your Mama showed me was that just because I never learned to read and write didn't mean I was dumb, just that I'd never had the proper opportunity.

"As soon as I caught sight of your mama I knew I wanted her to think of me as being important, even if I was an illiterate baseball-playing gandy dancer, who happened to be sent out to the prairies of South Dakota to put her railroad train back on the track.

"Your mama, she saw right through me. I've told you how after I met your mama, and after we got the railroad train back on the track, I quit my job as a gandy dancer and used most of my money to buy a ticket to Butte, Montana, which is where your mama was on her way to.

"Well, the first time we were in the dining car your mama caught me out. I always waited until the dining car or restaurant was full and then I'd pretend to read the menu, but I really looked around until I saw somebody eating something that looked good, and I'd say to the waiter, 'I'll have me some of that.'

"We were about half-way through our first meal together in the dining car of that train on the way to Butte, Montana, when your mama said to me, out of the clear blue, 'I ain't gonna marry me a man who can't read.'

"I had hardly even dared to think about marrying your mama, let alone asking her to marry me, though I knew I was going to, because I wasn't in the habit of quitting a job as a gandy dancer and leaving a baseball team in the lurch, and jumping on a train for Butte, Montana, on a minute's notice to chase after a girl I wasn't planning on marrying. I'd even had to leave my baseball glove behind; the glove that more or less made a living for me and I hadn't been parted from since I come home from the First World War. I made one of my fellow gandy-dancer-baseball-players promise to mail my glove and uniform and shaving kit to General Delivery, Butte, Montana, and then I hopped that train, for I knew if I ever let your mama out of my sight, why, she'd probably get plumb away from me and I'd never see her again.

"Once we got to Butte, Montana, your mama got out some McGuffy Readers, and she'd make me sound out words, and I'd be sounding out c-a-t, and I'd be sounding out d-o-g, I'd be sounding out h-o-u-s-e, simple words that kids in first grade learn without even thinking.

"And when I'd come across a bigger word that I couldn't sound out so good, your mama would smile and say, 'I reckon if you was to get this one right, I might be inclined to kiss you.'

"Jamie, son, you're too young to fully appreciate the significance of that gesture, but just imagine if you have a word you can't quite master and your teacher promises you two Wildfire chocolate bars a day for a year if you was to get it right. That's the significance of the incentive your mama provided me.

"The whole process was kind of a miracle, Jamie. I discovered I could write down all sorts of strange things. Like, I wrote down 'My sister is a green pig.'

"I just sort of looked at that sentence laying there on the page, and I about laughed my guts out. There was something permanent about writing things down. When you speak, what you say dies on the breeze, but writing down, Jamie, that's a whole 'nother matter, almost forever. I want you to remember that, son. Writing down is permanent and almost forever.

"I suspect I learned to read and write as fast as anyone has ever done, though I admit that after I caught on I did intentionally malinger over a few longer words, so as to get to earn the proper incentive before sounding them out or spelling them out, or writing them out in a complete sentence with a subject, and an object, and verb, and if I wanted to get a hug *and* a kiss, a subordinate clause or two, complete with commas, periods, and capitals."

It's odd, I remember that story word for word but I can't recall anything of Daddy's lecture on sex education.

Before I fell asleep at Mr. Oppenheim's house that night, I had seen something in Mrs. Oppenheim's kitchen that impressed me greatly. Mrs. Oppenheim had a refrigerator, and inside the refrigerator were a half-dozen bottles of Orange Crush, little brown corrugated-looking bottles. In our family we had never bought but one bottle of soft drink at any time. I guessed that what with working two jobs, or at least getting paid for two jobs, Mr. Oppenheim was rich. And I decided that when I grew up and got married, I would have a refrigerator with at least six bottles of Orange Crush in it.

Chapter Seven

It seemed that there was a conspiracy against Daddy. As Daddy himself said, "Regardless of my intentions, I always seem to wind up a day late and a dollar short."

Nobody could ever say Daddy's intentions were not good. As far as I know, Daddy never did a truly nasty thing in his entire life; but it didn't matter that he had good intentions, a good heart, and a kind disposition. The weather didn't care about such things, and neither did luck or coincidence.

It seemed to me it was first of all the weather, then bad luck, and then coincidence that did Daddy in on almost every occasion, especially the occasion of transporting Mama to the University Hospital at the south end of the High Level Bridge in Edmonton. It must have been awful scary being a man with a family in deep rural Depression Alberta, having no money and no prospects of money, and having no transportation other than horse and wagon or horse and buggy or just plain horse, and having a wife that had to be transported through what Daddy called "our annual biblical flood," just to get to a gravel road that passed for a highway which eventually led to the University Hospital in Edmonton.

When the snow melted, Jamie O'Day Creek covered most of our quarter-section with several inches of water and covered about two miles of what sometimes passed as a trail but never as a road with several inches of water in the level spots and several feet of water in the low spots, which when flooded seemed more numerous than when the weather was dry.

The snowfall had been heavier than usual, and once the snow melted it rained, long days of driving, dreary, needle-like rain that swelled the creek and deepened the brownish water that covered the land.

Mama's time approached and Jamie O'Day Creek didn't recede.

Mama was for using the team, Barney and Babe, and the wagon. Daddy owned a wagon with a rectangular wood box, that had four wheels with wooden spokes and steel treads, just like the ones that people whitewash and put at the end of their driveways as decorations in present-day civilization.

"The water can't be more than four feet deep at its worst," Mama said. "The horses are tall and strong and they can pull the wagon through to the highway, and the wagon box is high enough off the ground we won't get nothing more than our feet wet."

Daddy, while admitting that Mama had an idea, was for analyzing the situation thoroughly before making a decision. Daddy considered a boat. And a raft. And a windwagon. Daddy claimed to have seen a windwagon in Montana, and since the wind blows steadily and forever in Alberta, just like it blows steadily and forever in Montana, Daddy thought a windwagon would be a perfect means of transportation.

"A windwagon," Daddy said, "is simply a covered wagon with a sail, and the power of the wind carries it majestically across the prairies like a galleon."

"A windwagon would be alright if you were only traveling east, and if you were never coming back, and if the land around here was as flat as Montana," Mama said, though Mama also insisted that there was no such thing as a windwagon, and whatever Daddy had seen in Montana it was certainly not a windwagon.

After several evenings of sitting at the oilcloth-covered kitchen table drawing diagrams in one of my school notebooks, Daddy decided on a combination boat and windwagon, having decided that a genuine windwagon, propelled only by wind, would be apt to get stuck in the muddy fields, hung up on low-slung poplar, spruce, willow, or cottonwood trees, or encounter a hill too steep to navigate.

Daddy spent a whole morning waterproofing the wagon box. He heated up tar and creosote and the air was spicy with heat and sinus-clearing odors. After the tar had dried, Daddy drove the wagon to a point where the water lapped at the hubs of the big, spoked wheels and undid whatever it was held the wagon box on in the first place. Sure enough, the wagon box floated just like a boat. Daddy then fixed up what he called a tiller, which consisted of a tamarack pole and some binder canvas, and he scratched his head and looked pleased because he had, he figured, a wheelless windwagon on his hands.

"Or a sailboat," said Mama, "depending on how you look at it."

That deflated Daddy slightly, for it had never crossed his mind that he might be building something as mundane as a sailboat, but he still planned to test his invention. He and I set out to float the wheelless windwagon from a slough just south of our house to wherever it would go, which turned out to be not far. We had to stand stock still in the middle of the wagon box, for if we moved to either end, that end would dip and come in contact with the earth or with red willows and wild rose bushes.

A few yards into the voyage Daddy accidentally hit me along-side the head with the tiller, which caused me a certain amount of pain and knocked me flat on my bottom, where I quickly dis-covered that the wagon box was not as waterproof as Daddy had suspected, and the motion of the vehicle caused my cow-ardly dog Benito Mussolini to upchuck his breakfast.

The wheelless windwagon bogged down on an uphill slope about a quarter-mile south of the house, and Daddy had to get himself extremely wet, first carrying me and then my cowardly dog Benito Mussolini to safety. Then he had to hitch up Barney and Babe, hook them onto the wagon box and skid it back to the farm yard.

"Rafts are lightweight and move with the current," Daddy said.

He spent two evenings at the oilcloth-covered kitchen table, making drawings of a raft that, pictured from above, appeared about the area of Delaware. The raft had a lean-to on it and a cook stove. A tall, well-built man was poling the raft down a tranquil stream, while the man's pregnant wife, small son, and the small son's cowardly dog stood proudly beside him. Even as an artist Daddy was optimistic.

There was a stack of creosoted railroad ties around back of the horse barn that had been salvaged when the railroad that ran past Fark and other points in the Six Towns Area had been aban-doned. Daddy had hesitated to use those railroad ties as fire-wood, and hesitated to use them as a retaining wall for the garden, and hesitated to use them to replace the back wall of the chicken house when it collapsed, always remarking that someday those creosoted railroad ties were really going to come in handy.

Daddy carried them, one by one, down to the slough at the foot of the garden, and lashed about two dozen of them together with baling wire, hay wire, pieces of rope, and binder twine. Then Daddy cut himself a stout tamarack pole, which he said he would use to guide the raft, and hitched our old roan horse, Ethan Allen, to the raft and made Ethan Allen drag the raft into the deepest part of the slough, while Daddy stood on the raft that didn't look the least bit like the picture he had drawn, and prepared, as he put it, to become captain of his fate.

The raft sank like a rock, leaving Daddy standing up to his armpits in water, holding his stout tamarack pole over his head, and pulling on the reins to make Ethan Allen head back to shore before the water got any higher on Daddy.

I glanced toward the house about then, and I saw Mama's head disappear quick behind the white curtains on her and Daddy's bedroom window.

While his clothes were drying out over makeshift clothes lines in the kitchen, Daddy sat at the oilcloth-covered kitchen table in his full-length, grits-colored Stanfield's underwear for a considerable amount of time with his head buried in a volume of our encyclopedia, which had one volume missing, Daddy and Mama each having a different explanation for how that one volume got missing.

Daddy said the failure of the raft had to do with the specific density of the railroad ties, though he didn't attempt to elaborate, which meant Daddy was only passing certain of what he was saying.

"If at first you don't succeed," Daddy said. One of his favorite stories he liked to tell me almost every time I decided to quit a task unfinished was about somebody named Robert The Bruce. I could never bring myself to ask why Robert Bruce had *The* for a middle name, in case I would look really foolish. Robert The Bruce was losing some big battle or other when he got to watching a spider building his web, and was so impressed by the spider's tenacity that he said to his followers "If at first you don't succeed, try, try, again," and Robert The Bruce won whatever it was he was trying to win and became famous, because he'd be about nine hundred years old if he was alive.

Daddy decided that light was the way to go. Daddy went down to a pile of cut tamarack that was drying out for firewood, and he chose about two dozen tamarack poles, each about four inches across, and he sawed them into six-foot lengths.

That night Daddy drew some more diagrams in my school notebook. The raft was no longer the size of Delaware, but only about twice as big as the oilcloth-covered table Daddy was working at, and the lean-to was gone, the cook stove was gone, the small son and the small son's cowardly dog were gone. There was only a well-built man and the man's pregnant wife on the raft streamlined, Daddy said, for speed and maneuverability.

Daddy was able to hitch a rope to the raft and drag it to the slough himself. When that tamarack raft floated, Daddy was ecstatic. Daddy reckoned if he placed a pig in a wooden cage (we still had a few pigs, but they stayed in a pen at the side of the horse barn and got fed grain, so their fences didn't have to get shifted about the farm yard), he could raft the pig and the cage down Jamie O'Day Creek to within a quarter-mile of Fark and market during the flood season, and not have to wait until the land dried out.

The raft floated so well Daddy had to drive a post into the ground and tether it so it wouldn't float away of its own accord.

Daddy decided he would make a trial run to test the current, he said, downstream to Bear Lundquist's, where the flood more or less ended, and where Mama could ride in the back seat of Bear Lundquist's inherited 1941 Pontiac Silverstreak to the highway, while Bear Lundquist's only son, Ole Lundquist, followed along with his team of bays and pulled the Pontiac out of the mud when it got stuck, which would be maybe fifteen times between Bear Lundquist's farm and the Edmonton–Jasper Highway.

"Stay in the house," Daddy said. "This is man's work."

From Daddy and Mama's bedroom window there was a clear view of the slough and the raft, and Daddy hefting his long tamarack pole over his head, untethering the raft and poling it out into the middle of the slough, to catch the current that would carry him all the way to Bear Lundquist's.

My cowardly dog Benito Mussolini had somehow gotten onto the raft, and as Daddy shoved off, Benito Mussolini stood beside Daddy, all four legs stiff, as if the joints had been welded, and I could tell even from such a distance that my cowardly dog was even more terrified than usual.

Almost immediately, Mama and I were able to spot a major problem, though I don't think Daddy noticed it right away, he being so ecstatic that the raft was actually floating, and when he pushed off, the raft actually swung out to the middle of the slough and was probably picking up the current of Jamie O'Day Creek. The major problem Mama and I spotted was that the raft had disappeared; water was up past the ankles of Daddy's gumboots and almost up to Benito Mussolini's belly, and Benito Mussolini was, in his usually cowardly fashion, upchucking his breakfast.

"I expect your daddy will find the problem has something to do with weights and measures," Mama said.

The problem was that once Daddy and Benito Mussolini were on it, the raft sank about a foot below water level, while still moving to the center of the slough and catching the current of Jamie O'Day Creek.

When the water flooded over the top of Daddy's gumboots, he looked down and discovered his raft, built for speed and maneuverability, had disappeared. Daddy began trying to pole the unseen raft out of the current of Jamie O'Day Creek and get it back to safety at the edge of the slough.

"If we only had a camera," sighed Mama, who sometimes, when she was exasperated, said, not always in jest, that she ought to be equipped with a whip and a chair to deal with Daddy, with me, with Daddy's friends, and Daddy's extravagant plans. "Look there, he's walking on water. I always did wonder how that was done." And Mama smiled as pretty as I ever saw her smile. "Your daddy is a very special man," she said. "And don't you ever for a minute forget it."

Daddy poled and poled, but all the raft would do was turn in circles, depending on which way Daddy was poling, and edge a little further into the current every time Daddy relaxed. Finally, with a couple of mighty efforts Daddy pushed the invisible raft into the reeds at the back edge of the slough and studied the situation for a while, sitting on his haunches until the lapping water wet the bottom of his overalls and forced him to stand up. Daddy tried unsuccessfully to convince Benito Mussolini to swim to shore. Daddy finally gave up on Benito Mussolini and jumped off the raft, sinking to his armpits in water, and waded to shore. As soon as Daddy jumped off, the tamarack raft, built for speed and maneuverability, resurfaced, as if by magic, disengaged itself from the reeds, and swung back into the current, drifting slowly downstream in the direction of Fark and the Edmonton–Jasper Highway, Benito Mussolini dry-heaving, all four of his legs stiff as if the joints had been welded.

While his clothes were on the clothesline, Daddy sat at the kitchen table in a dry pair of Stanfield's underwear, with both my school notebook and the encyclopedia open on the table, contemplating his next move, which turned out to be searching for Benito Mussolini, because I made a considerable commotion, crying real tears and saying that if Daddy wouldn't go find my dog, I'd go find him myself. I would take my toy box, I said, and float down Jamie O'Day Creek until I caught up with Benito Mussolini and the tamarack raft.

It surprised me that I made such a fuss. Benito Mussolini was the most cowardly dog that ever lived, and I wasn't always that fond of him when he was around, but that was the trouble, I guess, Benito Mussolini was always around; and I loved him, even if he was stupid and cowardly and had whiskers that stuck out like a cat's and bad breath.

"The raft and the dog could have floated all the way to Purgatory Lake and the Pembina River by now," Daddy said, "and if he gets to the Pembina River why I reckon he'll end up eventually in Hudson Bay." Daddy then tried to assure me that Benito Mussolini wasn't so stupid that he wouldn't eventually jump off the raft and find his way home in an hour or two.

I pointed out between sobs that I didn't swim, and Benito Mussolini, never having anyone to set him an example, didn't swim either, and that if me or Daddy was on that raft we wouldn't jump off into deep water and neither would Benito Mussolini. I said I was going to get my toy box and set off after my dog, a bold-faced lie, for I was as scared of water as Benito Mussolini.

But I knew Daddy was soft-hearted, gullible, and a pushover for a sad story, and once Daddy's clothes were dry, he decided to conduct the search on his own.

Daddy reluctantly admitted, as he was getting dressed, that he had a certain fondness for Benito Mussolini, even if the dog was stupid and cowardly, afraid of cats, birds, and inanimate objects. And Mama, who had always been Benito Mussolini's harshest critic, claiming he ate twice as much as he was worth and that he shed even in rooms he wasn't allowed into, brought ticks into the house, tracked mud on her clean floors, and wasn't even a good watch dog, reckoned she might open up a sealer of canned chicken and give Benito Mussolini a small treat, if and when he returned home.

Daddy saddled up our old roan horse, Ethan Allen, and trying to stay on high ground, headed off in the direction the raft had disappeared, Ethan Allen having to plunge against the water, even when on high ground. He was back within an hour. Ethan Allen came plunging right down the the creek, part galloping and part swimming, and Daddy waved at us, Benito

Mussolini across the front of the saddle, the way a cowboy might carry a lost calf.

Daddy said he found Benito Mussolini about a mile away, right where Jamie O'Day Creek crossed the Correction Line. The raft had snagged on a pine tree, and Benito Mussolini was still standing on the raft with his legs stiff as if the joints had been welded and dry-heaving, and he wasn't showing any inclination to jump off the raft and swim to high ground like any intelligent dog would do.

We all agreed Benito Mussolini wasn't very intelligent, but we rubbed his ears as we said it, and Mama dried his head with a bath towel, something she wouldn't ordinarily have considered doing.

Mama wrapped both Daddy and Benito Mussolini in blankets and stuffed the cook stove with dry tamarack until it glowed pink as a rose petal. She opened a sealer of chicken, and we all, including Benito Mussolini, had jellied chicken and potatoes with lots of melted butter, pepper and salt. Mama said how nice it was to have all her family together, and she patted the belly of her dress when she said it, including my would-be brother or sister in the family.

When the time came for Mama to head for the University Hospital in Edmonton, and Jamie O'Day Creek still hadn't receded, Daddy, as Mama had originally suggested, hitched our team of blacks to the wagon and all three of us got in the wagon box and rumbled off, driving as much on high ground as possible, in the direction of Bear Lundquist's farm. There was only once that the water got so deep and the current got so strong there appeared a possibility that the wagon might get swept away. At that point Mama hung on to Daddy and Daddy hung on to the reins and I hung on to the edge of the wagon box.

We got to Bear Lundquist's with no more than four inches of water in the wagon box, and Bear Lundquist, coach and general manager of the Sangudo Mustangs baseball team, who was sixty-two years old and arthritic and always available to do a neighbor a good turn, fired up his inherited 1941 Pontiac Silverstreak, and Bear Lundquist's son Ole Lundquist harnessed up his team of bays, and with Mama safely in the back seat of the Pontiac, and me and Daddy in the front seat with Bear Lundquist, and Mrs. Bear Lundquist in the back seat with Mama and a picnic basket full of cold fried chicken, potato salad, and raspberry pie, drove as far as the Pontiac would go on what passed for a road. By alternating driving with pulling out of the mud, with a little picnicking during the pulling out of the mud part, we managed the few miles to the Edmonton–Jasper Highway in only six hours.

While Mama was waiting for the eastbound Western Trailways bus that stopped once a day at Bjornsen's Corner, who should come rumbling along the highway but Curly McClintock, with three of Wasyl Lakusta's yearling calves in the back of his dump truck, on his way to the Weiller and Williams Stockyards in Edmonton.

Curly said he'd be proud to transport Mama to Edmonton, and if she could wait while he made his first stop at the Edmonton City Dairy on 109th Street, he would be proud to transport Mama directly to the University Hospital.

After she had kissed me goodbye, Mama, with a little help from Daddy, and a little help from Bear Lundquist, climbed up into the cab of Curly McClintock's dump truck, after Curly had pushed aside several generators, a couple of brake shoes, miscellaneous hoses and gaskets, and a gallon jug of 10-30 motor oil that had only leaked a small amount on the seat. The truck cab smelled strongly of grease and oil, cigarette smoke, carbon monoxide, sour milk, and Curly McClintock. Mama made herself as comfortable as she could on the cold, greasy leather seat with springs poking through in several spots.

Mrs. Bear Lundquist handed up the picnic basket with what

was left of the cold fried chicken, potato salad, and raspberry pie, and after the truck backfired four or five times, and lurched twice, in spite of Curly McClintock letting the clutch out as carefully as possible, Mama was off to Edmonton to have her baby.

It was late evening before Daddy and I got back to the farm because it took just as long to retrace our route, with Bear Lundquist driving a ways and Ole Lundquist then pulling the Pontiac out of the mud with his team of bays.

For one of the few times in my life I was disappointed in Daddy that night, because right after we got home, right after Daddy stoked up the cook stove to warm the kitchen, he made me wash my face and hands, brush my teeth, and rewash my hands when he discovered that I had, as he put it, only rearranged the dirt.

My fantasy had been that with Mama away for a few days, Daddy and I would eat when we pleased, what we pleased — like toast and molasses for lunch and maybe chocolate corn starch pudding for supper — and that we would wash only when we pleased. I was especially looking forward to washing only when I pleased, because Mama was always hounding either me or Daddy to wash our hands, or me to wash my face, usually both before and after meals.

But Daddy was a thorough disappointment in that respect, for he made me wash just as much as Mama did, and he washed just as much as he ever did himself, and he kept the kitchen almost as neat as Mama, though he did tend to brush the toast crumbs off the table onto the floor, where Mama wiped them up with a wet dishcloth. His one concession to our bachelorhood was that at lunch time on about the third day, Daddy set three places at the table and allowed Benito Mussolini to sit in the third chair and eat his lunch off a plate just like me and Daddy.

I don't know as Benito Mussolini enjoyed his special treat all that much, for all through lunch he kept looking over his shoulder as if he expected Mama to suddenly appear and let out a cutlery-twanging yell, and maybe throw a piece of firewood at him as he scrambled under the kitchen couch.

"What Mama don't know, don't hurt her," Daddy said. "Don't you ever mention this to her, and you swear that dog to secrecy, too, y'hear?"

The next morning Daddy saddled up Ethan Allen and, heading west, away from Jamie O'Day Creek, with me bouncing uncomfortably behind the saddle and hanging onto Daddy's mackinaw with both hands, we rode to Oslin the Estonian's, where, while I played with the enveloping Oslins, Daddy collected the cradle for my soon-to-be brother or sister.

Daddy had once worked for a few weeks as a bricklayer, and, as he himself said, knew just enough about bricklaying to be dangerous. In return for the cradle, Daddy built a brick chimney in the middle of Oslin's slant-roofed shack. Daddy said as soon as times got better Oslin intended to build a large, two-story house around the brick chimney, to comfortably house all the enveloping Oslins, as well as any new little Oslins, and by the look of Mrs. Oslin a tenth enveloping Oslin was on the way.

The finished cradle was, Daddy said, a contradiction, for though the white birch was solid as rock, it was smooth as a flower petal to the touch. The Lamb of God bleated happily from either end of the cradle, its fluffy countenance looking, from a distance, like the real thing.

The brick chimney took well into the evening to finish, and Daddy and Oslin the Estonian and several of the enveloping Oslins were thoroughly covered in mortar by the time the project was finished, cutting into the already cramped space of the enveloping Oslins. When relative prosperity had returned to Alberta after the war, Oslin the Estonian moved his family away, and the shack eventually burned down in a grass fire, but I'm told that the chimney still stands, and that occasionally puzzled hunters stumble across it in a growth of white poplar and birch.

Daddy held the cradle in front of the saddle as we bounced along in the dark, dodging tree branches. At home, Daddy fumbled about in his and Mama's bedroom, sorting through some of my baby things and some of the presents Mama had received at her baby shower. He found some blue blankets and a rose-colored pillow, which, Daddy said, made the cradle presentable.

Daddy set the cradle in his and Mama's bedroom, and we walked around it a few times in the yellow lamplight, admiring the whiteness of it, admiring the Lamb of God on each end, and admiring the rose-colored pillow Daddy had placed on top of the blue blankets.

"We can alter the composition of the bedding as soon as we find out what kind of baby Mama's bringing home," Daddy said.

Then Daddy decided that the baby, at least until the weather got warm, which would be in a month or more, would spend most of its time in the kitchen, somewhere close to the cook stove. We moved the cradle to the kitchen, and Daddy set it on two chairs together alongside the reservoir, so the baby would be warm but spared the blast of heat from the front of the stove.

Over the next couple of days we admired the cradle while we waited for news from Mama.

When Mrs. Edina McClintock, widow of Black Darren McClintock, mother of Curly McClintock and mother-in-law to Gunhilda Gordonjensen McClintock, received the telephone message from the University Hospital in Edmonton, knowing that Jamie O'Day Creek was still above flood level, she had no idea of how to get the message to Daddy. Eventually, she wrote the message on a piece of paper and sent it with one of her grandchildren to Fark General Store, where Slow Andy McMahon was instructed to pass the message to Daddy if he should come to Fark for groceries.

Daddy went into Fark not only for groceries, but expecting a message from Mama, for Mama had agreed to phone Mrs. Edina McClintock as soon as she was well enough to get to a telephone. I bounced along behind the saddle, but at least I was short enough I didn't get my legs wet when Ethan Allen had to ford Jamie O'Day Creek.

As soon as Daddy read the note Slow Andy McMahon handed him, it was easy to tell Daddy was concerned, for he bought me a box of Cracker Jack and a bottle of Wynola to entertain myself with while he walked over to Mrs. Edina McClintock's to return the call to the University Hospital.

All Daddy said to me when he got back to the store was that things were not going as well as he and Mama had expected, and he was going to hitch a ride to Edmonton with Curly McClintock first thing in the morning. Daddy said it was not advisable for me to accompany him on the trip to Edmonton, and he said Mrs. Edina McClintock had graciously consented for me to stay with her while Daddy traveled to Edmonton. I knew things were not going well when Daddy talked formal like that.

Daddy also said that one of Edina McClintock's teenage boys, one of the ones who was a baby when Black Darren McClintock pushed back from the table after a feed of partridge parts and fried turnips, unbuckled his belt and passed away, was going to walk around Purgatory Lake to pay a call on Earl J. Rasmussen and arrange for Earl J. to travel to our house in order to milk our cow, Primrose, slop our hogs, feed our chickens and horses, and probably toss a few scraps to my cowardly dog, Benito Mussolini, who started to make the trip with us, but turned back the first time the water got so deep he was going to have to swim.

Earl J. Rasmussen reported later that as soon as the word of our tragedy made its way around the Six Towns Area, as always faster than pinkeye, several people showed up at our farm unsolicited to milk the cow, slop the hogs, feed the chickens and horses, and throw scraps to my cowardly dog, Benito Mussolini. Earl J. Rasmussen also reported several men from the Ukrainian community, led by Wasyl Lakusta, dropped by and replaced the back wall of the hen house.

I guess right from his telephone conversation with the University Hospital at the far south end of the High Level Bridge in Edmonton, Daddy knew most of the unhappy details, but he chose to keep me more or less in the dark, and let me, as Mrs. Edina McClintock said later, learn of the tragedy by degrees. And Daddy's strategy was for the best in the long run, for I don't think I would have wanted to know all at once that Mama had birthed a baby sister named Rosemary who, unfortunately, had something wrong with her heart and only lived for a little over twelve hours, and that Mama had taken the death of my baby sister very hard and was, as Daddy delicately put it to Mrs. Edina McClintock, not at all herself.

I stayed for several days with Mrs. Edina McClintock in what at one time had been the Fark Railway Station, a building now full of McClintocks: sons, daughters, in-laws and grandchildren, all of whom had an inordinate affinity for grease and oil. Daughters-in-law nursed babies at a table piled high with auto carburetors and distributor caps, while bigger babies crawled among the generators, bumpers, and grilles that littered the floor. All the babies seemed to chew on ballbearings, and if they swallowed a few it didn't seem to do them any harm.

On the fourth day Daddy telephoned, and he talked for a while to Mrs. Edina McClintock, a roll-yer-own tucked in the corner of her thin mouth, and then he talked to me, the first time in my life I talked on a telephone. Mrs. Edina McClintock handed the telephone to me and motioned for me to stand on a box so I would be tall enough to yell into the transmitter attached high on the wall of the kitchen.

I knew that long-distance telephone calls were for medical emergencies and deaths in the immediate family, so I knew before Daddy ever spoke that the news could not be good.

The first thing Daddy said was that he loved me and missed me, and then he said that Mama was alright, that she would be coming home with him in a few days, though her health was delicate and would be for some time.

I was surprised at Daddy's voice on the long-distance telephone, for though I had noticed that Mama sounded softly Southern when she spoke, I had never realized, until I heard Daddy's voice through the long distance-telephone wires, that Daddy had a severe Southern drawl.

I guess Daddy figured to sign off without discussing the baby, but I had been prepared ever since Daddy had made the first long-distance call to Edmonton, so I came right out and asked, "What about the baby?"

"I'm afraid I have some bad news," Daddy said, in his severe Southern drawl. "You had a baby sister named Rosemary, but she had something wrong with her heart and she only lived for twelve hours."

Daddy reassured me that Mama was fine, even though she was not quite herself and would be in a delicate state for some time, and I needed that reassurance, for last year the mama of the Waldemar Piska family had died while having a new baby, leaving behind a husband and four or five little Piskas. I was sorely worried the same was about to happen to Daddy and me.

It was several more days before Daddy and Mama came home on the westbound Western Trailways bus, and they were met by Mr. and Mrs. Bear Lundquist. I had spent my final three days at the Lundquists', where Mrs. Bear Lundquist plied me with huge cinnamon rolls and cups of cocoa cooked slow in a pan on the back of the stove. I wasn't allowed to meet the bus, and I guess I know why, for later on I heard Mrs. Bear Lundquist whisper that the baby, in a brown cardboard box, had accompanied Mama and Daddy, and had been unloaded like luggage from the bowels of the westbound Western Trailways bus, and was to be stored in the Lundquists' icehouse until the burying could be arranged.

Chapter Eight

The Bjornsens had donated a small parcel of land at the northern corner of their farm as a cemetery for the community of Fark, and that was where Rosemary was buried. There were eight or nine graves, only one with a granite marker, and that one in Ukrainian or Russian, the raised letters all off-angle and upside-down looking.

It surprised me that so many people turned out in the cold May drizzle for the funeral of a baby, but I guess they came for Mama and Daddy, both of whom were first to offer a helping hand when others were in trouble or suffered a loss.

Daddy and Mama had discussed the fact that they didn't want a preacher to conduct a service. That was about the only thing Mama had been able to make a concrete decision about since she came home, pale and empty-eyed. When she first saw me she looked at me for a fraction of a second as if I was a stranger turned up on her doorstep, maybe selling Raleigh Products or Fuller Brushes, a fraction of a second that scared me through and through, before Mama recognized me and reached her arms out to me.

Mama, Daddy pointed out, had to rest a lot, and wouldn't be able to concentrate very well for a while. Which was true. Mama would start to do one thing, then all of a sudden stop and start with another task, only to abandon that in a few minutes, pour herself a cup of coffee, and sit at the oilcloth-covered kitchen table and stare off into space, her face and eyes blank. She would fuss over me, wrapping me in too many clothes and forcing food on me, then spend a day or more ignoring me completely, not seeming to hear when I asked her something or told her something.

Not having a preacher conduct a service was more difficult than Mama and Daddy imagined. Pastor Ibsen of the Christ on the Cross Scandinavian Lutheran Church was the first to appear at our door, and we all noted that he had changed from his farming overalls to his shiny blue serge suit in order to make the call in his official capacity as sometime pastor. He carried a casserole of Norwegian meatballs prepared by his wife, offered his condolences, and offered to conduct the service for Rosemary either at the now semi-abandoned Christ on the Cross Scandinavian Lutheran Church in New Oslo, or at the Fark Community Hall, or at our house, not leaving Mama and Daddy many avenues of escape.

"We're not big on that sort of thing," Daddy said vaguely, trying to be diplomatic, get his own way, and not offend Pastor Ibsen, who was a kindly man with good intentions who had taken a morning off from his farming to pay us a condolence call.

"I quite understand if you have someone else doing the duties," Pastor Ibsen said, and I expect had Daddy left well enough alone the Pastor would have been on his way after a quick cup of coffee and a piece of Mrs. Edytha Rasmussen Bozniak's apple pie.

In cases of a death in the family there was a certain you might say competition among the families of the Six Towns Area to offer condolences and deliver food to the family of the deceased. In those days before electricity and the advent of refrigerators and freezers in the Six Towns Area, it is said that at least during the winter months, when about 80 per cent of the deaths occurred, several families — the Bear Lundquists, the Rasmussens, the Torval Imsdahls, to name a few — kept several apple and mincemeat pies and several cooked roasts of beef frozen in a block of ice, ready to be chipped out, heated up, and transported quickly to the family of the deceased, for there was a certain prestige in being first to pay a call of condolence.

Our first condolence call was, not surprisingly, from the widow, Mrs. Beatrice Ann Stevenson. Though Mrs. Irma Rasmussen and her daughter, Mrs. Edytha Rasmussen Bozniak, held that a condolence call could not be made until the whole grieving family were assembled under one roof, the widow, Mrs. Beatrice Ann Stevenson, had made her condolence call with a plate of roast beef sandwiches and some Icelandic desserts that had walnuts and maple sugar in them before Mama and Daddy had returned from the hospital in Edmonton, accompanied by the body of my baby sister. The condolence call had been paid on me at the Bear Lundquists', where the widow, Mrs. Beatrice Ann Stevenson, nearly smothered me in hugs and said she understood and sympathized with my great tragedy, and do have some food.

The first time we were alone in our big old house at the end of Nine Pin Road, Daddy thanked me for removing the crib from the house and hiding it in the hayloft of the barn.

"My heart was right up in my throat there," Daddy said, "for I had imagined it being the first thing your Mama saw when she walked in the door. Not something that would help her to a quick recovery."

On one of the days I spent with the Lundquists, I had walked a circuitous route to our house, where I put away the blue and pink blankets and baby clothes, and took the crib to the barn loft, a place Mama never went, and hid it under a pile of clover hay. The house was cold and scary, even in the middle of the day, and Mama's house plants were frozen black. I carried them outside and set them under the south window.

Daddy, in his dealing with Pastor Ibsen of the Christ on the Cross Scandinavian Lutheran Church, didn't leave well enough alone, for Daddy had a reputation among the men of the Six Towns Area for never being devious in a business deal, and Daddy considered having a preacher say a few words over his deceased daughter a matter of business.

"No," Daddy said, not leaving well enough alone, "we are not planning on having anyone else say a few words. In fact, we are not planning on having a religious service at all."

"But she was only a baby unwise in the ways of the world," Pastor Ibsen said, and I guess it was the way he said it, not so much sad that he wasn't going to get to conduct a service, but sad that Daddy didn't want one, that touched Daddy's heart.

"Hold on a minute," Daddy said, and he went into the bedroom where he and Mama conferred for a while, and I heard Mama's voice rise to twanging the cutlery for the first time since she came home from the hospital, but I couldn't make out the words, though I suspect she was chastising Daddy. *Gullible* was the word Mama usually used, for she was inclined to chastise Daddy frequently for being soft-hearted, gullible, and a pushover for a sad story, all of which even Daddy agreed he was.

Daddy eventually emerged from the bedroom and said that he supposed it would be alright for Pastor Ibsen of the Christ on the Cross Scandinavian Lutheran Church to say a few words at graveside, but graveside was the only place there was going to be a service, and would he be kind enough to keep it brief?

Pastor Ibsen smiled a kindly smile and allowed as how he would be charmed and delighted to perform a short graveside service, and after enjoying a quick cup of coffee and a slice of Mrs. Edytha Rasmussen Bozniak's apple pie with cinnamon, he went on his way.

Brother Bickerstaff of the Holy, Holy, Holy, Foursquare Brotherhood Church of Edson, Alberta, rode in on a borrowed bay gelding. Daddy said Brother Bickerstaff must surely have second sight, for Edson was a good sixty miles to the west and Brother Bickerstaff would have had to have a three-day start on the bad news to arrive so promptly.

Though in private Daddy allowed as how Brother Bickerstaff must be able to smell out heartache, when Brother Bickerstaff was present in his wide-brimmed white hat, white suit, and long black overcoat, Daddy allowed as how a few words from Brother Bickerstaff couldn't do all that much harm, and there was an outside chance they might lend comfort to someone present, but would Brother Bickerstaff be kind enough to keep his remarks brief, something Daddy knew was akin to asking a bird not to fly or a fish not to swim, for Brother Bickerstaff could emote for a quarter of an hour and not even touch on religious matters, upon someone remarking, "Nice day."

When several families from the Ukrainian community made a collective condolence call, they, just wanting to be helpful, brought along, standing like a scarecrow at the back of one of the wagon boxes, an itinerant Ukrainian Orthodox priest in his round black hat and long black cassock drizzled with food stains.

I remarked to Daddy that this Ukrainian Orthodox priest looked exactly like the Ukrainian Orthodox priest that had turned up at the wedding of Lavonia Lakusta and the Little American Soldier. Daddy said there was no way of telling, for all those fellows tended to dress and look alike. Not wanting to offend his Ukrainian friends, who were good neighbors and brought the best, tastiest, and most substantial food when they paid a condolence call, Daddy agreed it couldn't do any harm and would at least make the neighbors in the Ukrainian community feel good if the Ukrainian Orthodox priest said a few words over Rosemary. In private, Mama raised her voice to cutlery-twanging intensity for several minutes, which Daddy remarked to me later was good for her.

"It'll help her recovery to let off a certain amount of steam on matters not directly related to Rosemary's death."

For the baby's death, Daddy said to me, was in fact a major and catastrophic loss to Mama, a major but not so catastrophic a loss to Daddy himself, and a loss of undetermined nature to me. Daddy asked me how I felt about losing my baby sister, and I said I felt a little guilty that I didn't feel worse, and Daddy said I shouldn't feel that way, for after all I had never seen my baby sister, and she was more or less only a rumor that had once kicked my hand through Mama's belly; an expectation that went unfulfilled, Daddy said, as did most expectations in life.

I said I reckoned that if I had seen my baby sister, if she had curled her little hand around one of my fingers the way Oslin the Estonian's baby had done, or if I had got to kiss her little flat, baby nose the way all of us did to Oslin the Estonian's baby, then her passing would have been a catastrophic loss for me, too.

And just thinking about all those possibilities got the better of me, and even though I was big enough and old enough I didn't need to, I climbed into Daddy's lap and I cried for a long time, and Daddy took off the glasses he had been wearing to read the three-week-old *Toronto Star Weekly*, and tears sort of leaked out of his eyes and ran down his cheeks until he got out his big, red-checkered handkerchief and dried both our faces.

The day before the graveside service, through the mud left behind when Jamie O'Day Creek receded, came Earl J. Rasmussen's team and wagon, and perched on the seat of the wagon right beside Earl J. Rasmussen, was a genuine Catholic priest, with a wizened-up red face like a monkey.

Daddy had once, through no choice of his own, been a Catholic. He had, he said, escaped, though he was still hunted, and, like an escaped criminal, had to keep one eye always open and on the lookout.

"My sisters," Daddy said, and he tugged Mama's white, lemon-drop curtains all the way across the kitchen window, diminishing the light and shutting the Catholic priest from view, "did not even attempt to escape," though his youngest sister was said to smoke cigarettes in the privacy of her own home. Because they had not attempted escape, they took Daddy's escape personally, and spent a good part of their lives trying to convince Daddy he had made a mistake by choosing freedom of thought instead of the Catholic Church.

They spent money having the Catholic Church offer up prayers that were supposed to drag Daddy back into the fold, the very fact that people had to pay for prayers being one of the reasons Daddy said he had escaped, and they fairly deluged all three of us with tracts, Bibles, medals, and religious cards for all occasions, and they sent me jigsaw puzzles of the Last Supper, religious story books, David and Goliath dolls, and a little brown-velvet puppy with his back feet kneeling and his front paws in a position for prayer.

"Hysterical," Daddy called his sisters, my aunts, and said it was ideal for his closest sister to be about nine hundred miles away and the furthest over two thousand miles away.

"They're just like the law," Daddy said, peering cautiously from behind the curtains as Earl J. Rasmussen and the red-faced priest climbed down, "they track you to the ends of the earth."

The priest handed Earl J. Rasmussen several dollar bills. Earl J. Rasmussen would apologize to Daddy later, saying he just happened to be at Bjornsen's Corner when the priest emerged from the westbound Western Trailways bus, and that if he hadn't taken the priest's money, why, the priest would only have hired someone else to deliver him to the end of Nine Pin Road, and wouldn't Daddy rather have a friend like Earl J. get the money than a stranger? Or worse, someone who would do the job for free?

As the priest ambled a little unsteadily toward the door of our house, Earl J. Rasmussen decided he had serious business in the horse barn. Knowing Daddy's opinion of priests, he suspected he might be able to earn a few more dollars for a return trip to the Edmonton–Jasper Highway.

"They have a network," Daddy said, as we waited for the knock on the door. "One of your aunties must have let her priest know there was a death in our family; they probably used the telegraph or the long distance to pass the information. They still count me as a Catholic, and since I've got a family they count them, too. They are more stubborn than quack grass or the weather. Unrelenting is what they are."

The priest knocked.

"Why don't you keep your mama company," Daddy said.

Mama may or may not have been peeking out the bedroom window, but we both knew if she was, it was unwise for either of us to bother her until the situation was resolved. If she had seen the priest arriving, she would easily have recognized not only his purpose, but who sent him, and if she suspected he was going to soft-soap Daddy, who was soft-hearted and gullible even when he wasn't grieving the loss of a baby daughter, her voice would not only twang the cutlery but rattle the putty from about the window glass. There were, Mama once said, hard-shell Baptists back a generation or two in her family, but it was long enough ago that they were no longer tracked like animals in season.

Mama's religious philosophy was simple: If you live a decent life and treat people the way they deserve to be treated there is no place for pious folderol. And she would get away with saying that even to such religious fanatics as Mrs. Sven Bjornsen, because Mama did live a decent life and did treat people the way they deserved to be treated, and because of that she was genuinely liked by everyone, even those who disagreed with her religious philosophy.

I circled around behind the cook stove and squeezed into my favorite listening place beside the wood box.

The priest, whose name was Father Fryer (or maybe Friar), was not as fearsome as I would have guessed. He was not much older than Daddy, scrawny as a scarecrow, his face a polished, unhealthy red, and his right hand trembled when he raised his coffee cup to his mouth. Daddy, once he squared his back to the task of answering the door, where the priest and his past waited, was polite and hospitable, offering the priest coffee and his choice of condolence foods, and the priest chose some Norwegian fruitcake.

They spoke around the subject at hand for so long that I got downright drowsy, but eventually the priest made it clear he was present to officiate at the funeral of my baby sister, Rosemary. There was a very long pause after Daddy informed the priest that there was not going to be a funeral, only a graveside service, and Daddy didn't offer the priest any opportunity to participate.

While the priest was silent, I guess he was winding his springs and recalling the fine points of his vocation, picturing himself as a shepherd and Daddy as a lost sheep that had to be forced back into the fold come hell or high water.

The priest, once all his springs were wound, used the words *perdition, purgatory, mortal sin, innocent babe*, and ten or a thousand other words. He drank two cups of coffee, black, and ate four pieces of Norwegian fruitcake, frequently talking with his mouth full, occasionally spraying fruitcake crumbs across the table.

Daddy didn't say much, except that a man was entitled to his opinion. He let the priest have his full and complete say, which certainly was full and complete, but I could feel Daddy's resolve crumbling, blowing away on the wind of the priest's words. Daddy was probably deciding that since he had already been chastised by Mama for allowing Pastor Ibsen, Brother Bickerstaff, and the transient Ukrainian Orthodox priest to say a few words at the graveside, he might as well let the Catholic priest do the same, feeling that it might bring some comfort to those who shared the Catholic priest's views, and would certainly ease the torrent of letter-writing from his sisters in South Carolina and South Dakota.

Daddy being soft-hearted, gullible, and a pushover for a sad story, eventually interrupted to say he reckoned he could tolerate the priest saying a few words graveside, though the priest wasn't, come hell or high water, to conduct a full service.

The priest sighed deeply, breathing a few more Norwegian fruitcake crumbs across the table. He would be proud and happy to perform a graveside service for the poor, dear, innocent babe, thus assuring her immortality.

Daddy, too, heaved a sigh of relief, then went on to say he hoped the priest would keep his remarks short for he was sharing the graveside service with Pastor Ibsen, Brother Bickerstaff, and an itinerant Ukrainian Orthodox priest.

Well, the priest got even redder in the face, and forgot all about the windings of his springs, the fine points of his vocation, bringing the sheep back into the fold, and everything else except that he NEVER, and he emphasized the word by banging his trembling fist onto the oilcloth-covered kitchen table, sending Norwegian fruitcake crumbs dancing in the air, shared a service with any denomination. Such acts were heresy and forbidden by Rome, and he personally wouldn't share a service with such a scandalous bunch of heathens even if it *weren't* explicitly forbidden by Rome.

Daddy just stood up and pointed at the door, and the scrawny, mercurichrome-faced scarecrow of a priest muttered his way out the door to where Earl J. Rasmussen waited in the early May sunshine, astride the doghouse of my cowardly dog, Benito Mussolini.

The priest began to climb up onto Earl J. Rasmussen's wagon and motioned for Earl J. Rasmussen to go get his horse. Earl J. Rasmussen, who was never in a hurry to get anywhere, held up his hand like a policeman stopping traffic and said there was a certain amount of negotiating to do.

The priest, not in the best of moods, said he had already paid Earl J. Rasmussen what he assumed constituted a return fare.

Earl J. Rasmussen said he was a sheep farmer, not a taxi driver, and if the priest wanted to get back to Bjornsen's Corner, he had to cough up, enough dollars that the exact return fare, Earl J. Rasmussen calculated, would allow him to acquire a purebred ewe owned by a Hutterite farmer up near Glenevis.

The priest climbed down off Earl J. Rasmussen's wagon and said that he would walk to the next farm, where a man of the cloth might receive a friendlier welcome.

Earl J. Rasmussen pointed out the nearest farm was a long ways off by what were generously referred to as roads.

The priest eventually paid Earl J. Rasmussen enough to buy the purebred ewe from the Hutterite farmer up near Glenevis, and as they rumbled over what were generously referred to as roads in the direction of the Edmonton–Jasper Highway, Earl J. Rasmussen dreamed of flocks of purebred sheep and the priest dreamed of lost sheep never to be recaptured.

At the graveyard in a corner of a quarter-section owned by Sven Bjornsen of the Bjornsen Bros. Swinging Cowboy Musicmakers, a cold, steady May drizzle splattered our faces. In spite of the weather, almost everyone from the Six Towns Area was there, even Loretta Cake, leading eight square-jawed tom cats on leashes and dressed like a wet Sheena, Queen of the Jungle; even the infamous Flop Skaalrud, his blondish hair slicked down with Vaseline, standing at an advantageous angle so anyone who chose to be could be influenced by his blatant male aura.

"A funeral," Daddy had said earlier, "whether we like it or not, is a community event, just like a wedding or a box social. And just as a community feels deprived if a social event is canceled or if a wedding is moved outside the community, so they feel deprived if a funeral is canceled. We've declined to have a funeral, but for the sake of the community we have to hold a graveside service."

Mama said she couldn't see why, when we were the bereaved family, we should put ourselves out because someone else's nose would be out of joint if we didn't hold the proper kind of ceremony.

Daddy pointed out that someone else's grieving made people feel better about themselves, pointing out to them that there were people worse off than they were, and though they might be poor, badly clothed, badly housed, they still had their loved ones, unlike the people grieving.

Eventually, Mama said she would go along with a graveside service, providing it was kept short and sweet, though she knew in her heart that nothing done in the Six Towns Area was ever short and was only occasionally sweet.

There was a sizable contingent from the Ukrainian community both within and without the Six Towns Area, for our bereavement was a chance for them, just by showing up, to say thank you to my Daddy for all the times he had turned up to do chores when someone was sick, or given a hand with planting or harvesting, or building that extra room on the house or lean-to on the barn.

Since there was no one actually in charge of the graveside service, and since perhaps the itinerant Ukrainian Orthodox priest had someplace else to officiate, it was decided without a meeting or a vote that the Ukrainian Orthodox priest would go first. He climbed down off the back of Wasyl Lakusta's wagon box and stood himself at the foot of the grave, his little round black hat blotched with rain, his long black, food-drizzled cassock skimming the grass. There was a little pile of yellow gumbo had been scraped out of the ground by whoever dug the grave, probably one of the Bjornsens, since they lived closest — it was an honor to dig the grave, and each family attending the graveside service would have carried along a round-mouthed shovel in their wagon box in case it was needed.

As was the custom, the children of the Six Towns Area had scattered what wild flowers were available, yellow cowslips and a few crocuses, over the ugly diggings, and some had brought everlasting daisies of ivory, golden yellow, and Halloween orange that they'd collected the summer before for just such an occasion, looking natural, but dried and brittle as butterfly wings.

The Ukrainian Orthodox priest said a few words over the grave that the large contingent from the Ukrainian community understood, and possibly took comfort from. The rest of us didn't understand, except that the tone was universal, and, as though he understood the look Mama gave him, the Ukrainian Orthodox priest did keep his remarks mercifully short, then stepped back a couple of steps, while Mrs. Rose Lakusta's father, who was ninety-if-he-was-a-day, was set on a folding chair where he played the dobro and sang a funeral song, again, the tone being universal.

Brother Bickerstaff of the Holy, Holy, Holy, Foursquare Church was quicker on the draw than Reverend Ibsen, possibly because Brother Bickerstaff's church was thriving and Reverend Ibsen's was not.

Brother Bickerstaff, in spite of Daddy's request and Mama's insistence that he keep his part of the graveside service short, did not know the meaning of the word *short*. He launched into a fire-breathing sermon that didn't seem to have anything to do with the death of my baby sister, Rosemary, but had everything to do with converting the heathen, and if I interpreted correctly everyone except Brother Bickerstaff was a heathen when it came to the ways of the Lord.

Brother Bickerstaff delivered his fire-breathing sermon with, as Daddy said, the intensity of a good-old-fashioned, rattle-the-windows-and-scare-the-cattle Alberta electric thunder and lightning storm, snorting between each admonition, and pawing the earth like an agitated bull.

Mama looked pale, and smaller than I had ever seen her look; Mama had always looked like a giant to me before. She clung to Daddy's arm, but her eyes that had appeared so blank when she came home from the hospital now had a spark in them, and I thought that was good, even if it was a spark of rage at the endless rantings of Brother Bickerstaff, who was actually playing a part in Mama's recovery, but certainly not the part that he imagined.

Daddy could see Mama had taken about all that she could stand, and Daddy had taken about all he could stand, and probably everybody present had taken all they could stand. Daddy let go of Mama's hand, stepped to the foot of the grave, and held up his hand, cutting off Brother Bickerstaff in mid-rant.

"Thank you, Brother Bickerstaff," Daddy said. "I know you'll understand that we have other business to get to and a limited amount of time. Reverend Ibsen would now like to say a few words."

Brother Bickerstaff snorted one final time, and pawed the earth one final time, but he knew from the tone of Daddy's voice that Daddy was serious, and he vacated the preaching spot to Reverend Ibsen, a kind-hearted man with, as Daddy said, a closetful of good intentions, but not a good preacher, and only passably good at calling on his parishioners of an afternoon to enjoy a piece of Norwegian fruitcake and, if it was offered, a glass of dandelion wine.

Reverend Ibsen had for many years now been farming a worthless quarter-section of land, and he only dusted out the church and fired up the blue potbellied stove in its center on special occasions.

Before Reverend Ibsen began, the Bjornsen Bros. Swinging Cowboy Musicmakers, each carrying a three-foot-by-three-foot section of portable stage and their chosen instrument, minus the piano, walked the quarter-mile from their house to the grave-yard, wearing, as their concession to formality and solemnity, identical plaid shirts buttoned to the collar, and string ties. There was the jingle of harness from where teams of horses, tethered at the edge of the graveyard, chomped at the slips of new, green grass that needled its way up through the dry grasses from last fall.

Sven Bjornsen nodded and the Swinging Cowboy Musicmak-ers played "The Old Rugged Cross," one of three hymns they knew and played at each and every funeral in the Six Towns Area, and occasionally at a box social, community dance, or ethnic wedding when things got out of hand and a friendly dis-cussion had turned first to a disagreement, then to a shoving match, then to a fist fight, and finally to a genuine altercation. It was Sven Bjornsen's feeling that genuine altercations tended to slow down to an absolute crawl when choreographed to the rhythm of "The Old Rugged Cross."

Most everyone sang along with the Bjornsen Bros. Swinging Cowboy Musicmakers, the widow, Mrs. Beatrice Ann Steven-son, who said she was a natural contralto and with a little train-ing could have sung professionally, leading the way.

Oslin the Estonian and his family were there, Oslin the only one no more silent than usual. He had carpentered the casket from white birch as lovingly as he had created the sad little cradle still unknown to Mama, hidden in the hayloft, sanded and varnished so tenderly, the Lamb of God bleating at its head and foot.

Reverend Ibsen was mercifully brief, saying succinctly that in times of grief we took strength and courage from our friends, and that by the turnout today it was obvious that Johnny and Olivia and Jamie O'Day had a legion of friends, and he knew that he spoke for everybody present when he said that those friends were there to lean on and take courage from, not just today but every day of the year, and he sputtered just a bit before he said quietly that perhaps we should sing one more hymn and then disperse.

The Bjornsen Bros. Swinging Cowboy Musicmakers began their rendition of "Shall We Gather at the River?" which is easy to sing along with, and after that there was a lot of shaking hands and hugging and crying and I got my head patted about three thousand times and told about three thousand times what a big brave man I was, which was a lie, but wasn't awful to hear.

Most of us then walked away to a grove of cottonwood trees, where the women of the Six Towns Area had spread a picnic table with about a ton of food, and we ate and hugged and cried and listened to lies while dodging raindrops, and didn't watch as Wasyl Lakusta and Earl J. Rasmussen lowered the tiny coffin and filled in the grave, the live yellow cowslips and mauve crocuses and the dried everlasting daisies mixing with the wet yellow gumbo.

What I remember most clearly about the funeral were my father's friends: Earl J. Rasmussen, Wasyl Lakusta, Bear Lundquist, the infamous Flop Skaalrud, and a dozen more, usually so jovial but that day standing like stones circling the grave, uncomfortable men, their huge hands poking from unfamiliar sleeves, heads bowed, trying to comprehend; such helpless men, able to fix anything with a length of baling wire, except their children.

SECTION THREE

The Reconstituted Wedding

Chapter Nine

I have heard it argued that the debates that go on month after month, year after year, sometimes even generation after generation, that accelerate from mere time-passing conversation to arguments, to disagreements, to shoving matches, to fist fights, to genuine altercations, and occasionally to an outright brouhaha resulting in bent cartilage of the proboscis and blood-spots on a Sunday shirt, are both impractical and impossible, and since the argument usually involves a time or a date, could be settled once and for all by a minimum of research.

No one will dispute impractical, but impossible, certainly not, and a minimum of research was not an alternative in the Six Towns Area.

Like the time Knut Knutsen and Knut Osbaldson were sitting in front of the New Oslo General Store, both balanced somewhat precariously on the peeled pine hitching post. Knut Knutsen pronounced the *k*s in both his names, while Knut Osbaldson didn't pronounce his one *k*, and he refused to pronounce the two *k*s assigned to Knut Knutsen, whose name Knut Osbaldson pronounced Noot Nootsen, the mispronunciation considered by Knut Knutsen to be just an idiosyncrasy though Knut Osbaldson claimed that people who pronounced the *k*s in either "Knut" or "Knutsen" were Swedish and not Norwegian, and that since a Swede was a Norwegian with his brains knocked out, the pronunciation of the *k*s was a fatal mistake nationalistically speaking. The *k* in knocked, he argued, was also silent, just like the *k*s in Knut and Knutsen, when properly pronounced.

What set Knut and Knut a'going was that in connection with some incidental matter Knut Knutsen happened to say, "I do remember it because it took place the same February as Gunnar Johanson's funeral, and I was standing beside Elsie Rolvang at Gunnar Johanson's funeral."

That statement was like lighting a fire under Knut Osbaldson, for he then said to Knut Knutsen, "It just goes to show you don't remember even the simplest information that anybody else would recall, because Elsie Rolvang had been dead for a full six months before Gunnar Johanson passed to his reward — Elsie Rolvang died in the summer of '37 and Gunnar Johanson passed to his reward in February of '38, the twelfth of the month if I'm not mistaken."

At this point the original matter was forgotten, as Knut Knutsen set out to prove he had stood beside Elsie Rolvang at Gunnar Johanson's funeral.

"The reason I know Elsie Rolvang was alive and well and in attendance at Gunnar Johanson's funeral is because of what she was wearing on her head. As everyone knows, even you, I assume, Elsie Rolvang, after her last illness, was left all but bald-headed, and in order to make herself presentable for public appearances she took to wearing one of those turbans, the likes of which were worn by these here East Indian people and that little fellow Secundra Das in the novel by Robert Louis

Stevenson, the title of which escapes me at the moment, but which I studied in seventh grade in Duluth, Minnesota, a good number of years ago.

"The reason I remember that Elsie Rolvang was alive and well, or at least as well as could be expected, and in person at Gunnar Johanson's funeral in February of 1938, the twelfth of the month if I'm not mistaken his death that is, the funeral was a day or two later, was that she had purchased, probably specifically for Gunnar Johanson's funeral, a white scarf of a particularly slick silk material, and when she had tried to wrap that slick silk scarf around her all-but-bald head into a genuine turban, it ended up down over her nose or bunched along the back of her neck.

"Now what Elsie Rolvang had done in order to give the slick silk scarf something to cling to other than her all-but-bald head, was to borrow her husband Ole's green John Deere cap with the yellow embroidery on the crown — you'll remember, if you have half as good a memory as I do, that we used to joke with Ole Rolvang that he had snatched poor old Elsie bald-headed, though no one ever made mention of her all-but-bald head within her hearing — and what she did with that green John Deere cap with the yellow embroidery on the crown was to put it on backward, just like a baseball catcher and then wind that slick silk scarf around her all-but-bald head in order to form a genuine turban.

"The reason I remember Elsie Rolvang being alive and well and at Gunnar Johanson's funeral was that I was standing not exactly beside her, but beside and a half a step behind her, so I was able to admire that slick silk turban, but I was also able to see, peeking from underneath the genuine turban like these here East Indian people wear, the green bill of Ole Rolvang's John Deere cap showing between the end of the turban and the collar of her coat."

"I'm not denying," said Knut Osbaldson, who was, after listening to that long explanation, borderline disgruntled, "that you stood beside Elsie Rolvang at somebody's funeral, though certainly not Gunnar Johanson's funeral, and noticed that she had worn her husband Ole's green John Deere cap backwards over her all-but-bald head and under her slick white silk turban just like these here East Indian people wear, though I'm unfamiliar with the literary character you mention, and, if you'll recall the colored comics from the *Toronto Star Weekly*, you'll remember that there is a fellow named Punjab in that *Little Orphan Annie* comic strip who also wears a genuine turban and would have served just as well as an example without putting on literary airs."

The argument continued back and forth, never accelerating to shoving match, fist fight, genuine altercation, or outright brouhaha, though an argument like that could smoulder like a ground fire for days, weeks, or even months before it would suddenly flare up again when Knut Knutsen and Knut Osbaldson met at the hitching rail in front of Fark General Store, though when given the opportunity, such as when both attended the burial of another friend or acquaintance, neither would check the gravestone of Gunnar Johanson or of Elsie Rolvang, and the argument would continue sporadically, like thunder showers, until one of the combatants cashed in and the other declared himself the winner, though in some cases the argument could pass from generation to generation if the combatants had heirs of suitable age and temperament.

The winter Helen dropped by, which was followed by the summer Jamie damn near drowned, though that summer was actually a spring, was preceded by the summer my daddy took on the case of Lousy Louise Kortgaard versus the Province of Alberta.

"Your daddy," Mama was known to say frequently, "has a highly developed sense of right and wrong." Then Mama would smile, kind of turning her lips inward when she did so. "Not that having a highly developed sense of right and wrong is entirely negative," Mama would go on, "though I do wish your daddy would choose his causes more carefully."

What set my daddy off was the fact that a number of boys, a few years older than me but boys nevertheless, were making fun of Lousy Louise Kortgaard at the break-up of the outdoor dance that followed the Doreen Beach Sports Day and Picnic, ill-fated fireworks, burning of the Doreen Beach Community Hall (the reason for the outdoor dance), and the almost-burning of Slow Andy McMahon, all three hundred and some pounds of him.

"I will skin you alive if you do anything like that when you're older," my daddy said to me, as the buggy, pulled by our old roan horse Ethan Allen, was passing the group of boys making fun of Lousy Louise Kortgaard.

Lousy Louise, Daddy explained, was not named because there were any cooties in the Kortgaard household, or any cooties on Lousy Louise herself. The Kortgaards were law-abiding Norwegians who came to Canada later than most of the families in the Six Towns Area and spoke more Norwegian and less English than most, and it was less English that got Lousy Louise in difficulty. "And it was," Daddy said, "the arrogance and stupidity of the Government of Alberta, Bureau of Vital Statistics, that allowed that difficulty to continue.

"Vital statistics," Daddy went on, "were not of importance to immigrant farmers digging out a living on bad land during the Great Depression, and government agencies have the collective intelligence of a dead newt."

Until I was somewhat older I thought Daddy was saying a dead Knut, as in Knut Osbaldson or Knut Knutsen or Knut Ibsen, son of Pastor Ibsen of the Christ on the Cross Scandinavian Lutheran Church. Knut Ibsen, as my rabbit-snaring buddy Floyd Wicker and the Osbaldson twins from over by Purgatory

Lake could testify, had some highly peculiar ideas about what constituted fun when two boys were playing together without adult supervision. Later, Knut Ibsen, who had been born with the *k* silent, decided to pronounce the *k* and became known as Mr. Knut, of Mr. Knut's Hairstyling and Permanent Wave Salon, on l24th Street, just north of Jasper Avenue, the first male, or at least mostly male, hairdresser in Edmonton.

Although most babies in the Six Towns Area were born at home, Mama reportedly said to Daddy about seventh months into building me, "We may be down but we are not out, and we may be poor but we have not abdicated our humanity, and though I may have to bear the cruel punishment of living in proximity to a town called Fark, I will not have my child born in the wilderness with a bunch of people standing around who may or may not know what they are doing, so, Johnny O'Day, you had better do something about it."

The weather helped Daddy do something about it, because a humdinger of a freeze-the-balls-off-a-brass-monkey Alberta blizzard came along right after Mama's proclamation, and Daddy got six days' work driving the county snowplow, earning just enough to send Mama in Curly McClintock's inherited dump truck to Edmonton when she showed the first signs of my approaching birth.

I was registered with the Government of Alberta, Department of Vital Statistics, as James Oliver Curwood O'Day, named for a man who wrote a book called *The Valley of Silent Men*.

Lousy Louise Kortgaard was the third of seven Kortgaards born at the Kortgaard homestead in the area of Doreen Beach, none of whom were registered with the government.

When the first two got old enough to start school, Miss Quick, the teacher at Fark Schoolhouse, started them off in grade one and taught them to read, write, count, and wipe their noses, but the year before Louise Kortgaard was to start school, the Government of Alberta decided that no more little Kort-gaards or little Anybody-at-alls could begin first grade unless they had a genuine birth certificate to prove their existence. There were forms to be filled out and sent to the Department of Vital Statistics with a fifty-cent fee.

Bjorn Kortgaard was a man with not much education in Nor-way and none in Canada, a hard-working man fighting a losing battle against bad land and the Great Depression. With the help of his two sons, one in first grade and one in second grade, he filled out the form to get little Louise a birth certificate.

They did fine with KORTGAARD, even remembering the double *a*. They did passing well on LOUISE, except they left out the *i*.

When Louise Kortgaard enrolled in first grade at Fark School-house, Miss Quick, who could spot a spelling mistake from a hundred yards, noticed it, but not before several of the older stu-dents had determined that Louise Kortgaard was registered with the Government of Alberta as Louse Kortgaard.

Miss Quick simply changed the word *Louse* to *Louise* on the class register, and it took until almost Christmas before the Gov-ernment of Alberta wrote to Miss Quick pointing out that she didn't have the authority to alter a student's name from the birth certificate version, and Louise would remain Louse Kort-gaard until, as Miss Quick said, the cows came home.

"That poor little girl is going to be known to her dying day as Lousy Louise Kortgaard, unless someone does something about it," Daddy said, when he witnessed the boys tormenting Louise after the July 4th Sports Day and Celebration at Doreen Beach, and the burning of the Doreen Beach Community Hall.

"Do you know what an oxymoron is?" my daddy asked as we chugged along the Edmonton–Jasper Highway in Curly McClin-tock's inherited dump truck toward Edmonton.

"I don't have any idea," I said.

"Is it some kind of soup?" asked Curly McClintock.

"No," said Daddy, "and it ain't a particularly stupid ox either, though Lord knows an ox is stupid enough for two of anything else. No," Daddy went on, "an oxymoron is a contradiction in terms. The second most obvious example is 'military intelligence.' Today we are going to encounter the most obvious, the 'civil service.' "

Curly McClintock dropped us off at 109th Street and Jasper Avenue, and we walked about a mile down 109th Street until, just before the High Level Bridge, we were confronted by the Alberta Parliament Buildings, all made of marble — floors, pillars, staircases — and smelling like old newspapers, varnish, and the green soap in public restrooms.

We rode the elevator to the third floor.

On one of the heavy oak doors were the words, Department of Vital Statistics. The door said, Walk In, which we did.

Daddy leaned on a varnished wooden counter.

Behind the counter, as far as the eye could see, all the way to the back wall, were desks about two or three feet apart, and each desk was identical, and at each desk was a civil servant, and as far as I could see each civil servant was identical.

After Daddy had been leaning on the counter for a spell, one of the identical civil servants in the second row stood up, very slowly, and walked to the counter.

"May I be of service?" said the identical civil servant, whose skin was the exact gray color of his suit and who had a long, sad face like an old dog, with watery eyes and pale hair.

"I reckon you may be," Daddy said, and produced Louise's birth certificate, which he had collected by stopping by the Kortgaard farm and saying "I've got me some business to do in Edmonton, and I'd be proud to take little Louise's birth certificate along and get her name spelled proper."

"As you can see," Daddy said to the identical civil servant, "this little girl's name got misspelled, and it got misspelled in such a way that it causes her grief and will continue to cause her grief if the mistake ain't rectified. Do you think you could see your way clear to take care of it?"

"The Government of Alberta does not misspell," said the identical civil servant. "We simply record. If the information given us to record is incorrect, that is the fault of the applicant. We will, however, in due course, if the information is processed through proper channels, correct *your* mistake."

The identical civil servant said all that in a mosquito-like whine.

"Well," said Daddy, almost smiling, "suppose we start the wheels in motion to correct this here mistake."

"Suppose we do," said the identical civil servant, looking down his nose at Daddy. "I will get the file. Have a seat." And the identical civil servant motioned at the brown-varnished bench just inside the door.

The identical civil servant then spent an inordinate amount of time filling out a form, three copies without carbon paper, and deposited one copy in a filing cabinet at the far end of the room, stopping on the way to jaw for a lengthy spell, put a second copy in the middle of the green blotter on his desk, and rolled up the third copy like a biblical scroll and dropped it into a cylinder, and opened up a slot in the wall and rammed the cylinder in the slot, and there was a whooshing sound.

The identical civil servant then went back to his desk and sat with his hands folded on his copy of the form and waited.

Daddy and me sat on the varnished bench just inside the door, twiddled our thumbs, sometimes in unison, and waited.

After the better part of an hour, there was a whooshing sound and a cylinder knocked at the glass door in the wall. After lengthy consideration, the identical civil servant unfolded his hands from the copy in the middle of his desk and made his way to the glass door where he retrieved the cylinder, emptied it out, carried the papers back to his desk and studied them for the better part of half an hour before walking slowly to the counter.

"I believe we have the beginnings of the required paperwork here to correct *your* mistake, Mr. Kortgaard. Now, if you'll just sign here."

He pushed the paper toward Daddy.

I could tell by the look on Daddy's face that he wanted to lie, but Daddy, as Mama repeatedly said, had a highly developed sense of right and wrong, and knew that it would be wrong to lie, and had told me a few hundred times that "honesty is the best policy," and wished he had added "except when dealing with oxymorons." I could also tell from my brief exposure to the identical civil servant that he and his kind needed to be lied to, and I looked at Daddy, hoping to convey my thoughts to him. I wanted to let Daddy know I understood the circumstances. I understood that these oxymorons in the civil service would always find something about the truth unacceptable.

"Mr. Kortgaard, sir," I said, loud enough to attract the attention of the identical civil servant, "why don't you just go ahead and fill out that form to correct the spelling of your daughter's name."

Daddy looked startled.

"Mr. Kortgaard can't write anything in English except his name, which is how come he made the mistake."

The identical civil servant pushed the form a couple of inches closer to Daddy, and Daddy signed the form.

He hugged me about ten times as we were walking out of the Parliament Buildings, and he allowed as how if we walked about ten blocks we'd be at the Woolworth's Five and Dime Store where they sold hot dogs for five cents, and where I was welcome to eat as many as I could comfortably hold.

Chapter Ten

"If the Donner Party had been given that meal," my mama said, "they'd have still eaten each other, it was that bad."

In our buggy, pulled by our old roan horse, Ethan Allen, we were just driving away from the home of the widow, Mrs. Beatrice Ann Stevenson.

"Some of the saddest food this side of an A-rab bazaar," Daddy added. Daddy, traveling around after the First World War, claimed to have seen an A-rab bazaar where they sold goats' eyes from a bucket and, Daddy said, the flies crawling on the goats' eyes were about as big as the goats' eyes themselves.

The food Mama and Daddy were talking about had just been served to us by the widow, Mrs. Beatrice Ann Stevenson, who was historically, Daddy said, a very good cook. The reason the food was so bad was that the very evening before, the widow, Mrs. Beatrice Ann Stevenson, had finally accepted the proposal of Daddy's friend Earl J. Rasmussen, who had been courting the widow for as long as I could remember, letting her know frequently and in no uncertain terms that he was hers for the taking.

"I am so flustered I can't cook straight," is exactly what she said while she was cooking supper. Mama did admit while on the way home that the unpalatable food, which may or may not have been mutton, was our own fault for dropping in unannounced, although Mama admitted there really was no way not to drop in unannounced, since only three families in the Six Towns Area had telephones and only two of those telephones worked, and since folks only picked up their mail every so often it didn't do much good to send a letter.

The widow, Mrs. Beatrice Ann Stevenson, as well as being flustered, was, according to her own account, all aflutter as well. She said it was just so romantic that Earl J. Rasmussen had proposed after she had cooked him up a feed of pork chops, potatoes, turnips with country gravy, spinach greens with malt vinegar, both green and yellow buttered beans, beet pickles and corn relish, apple cobbler with whipped cream, and Chase and Sanborn coffee.

Mama said she supposed the widow, Mrs. Beatrice Ann Stevenson, could be forgiven for being flustered and all aflutter, though the proposal shouldn't have come as much of a surprise, for Earl J. Rasmussen had been proposing to the widow an average of once a week for at least ten years, and the only thing that must have changed was the way the widow viewed the proposal.

Mama said she supposed it was quite alright for the widow to be flustered and all aflutter, for, after all, she had spent the better part of her life being a widow and hardly any being a wife. Mama said that the widow, Mrs. Beatrice Ann Stevenson, was originally a Birkland from Camrose, and had attended to tenth grade at Camrose Lutheran College before she met Alf Stevenson, whose father worked for the United Grain Growers elevator in Camrose, and whose family was related to the famous

Icelandic poet Stephan G. Stephansson, their family name having been altered to Stevenson by an immigration official.

The former Beatrice Ann Birkland was happy to become Icelandic by marriage and was happy when her father-in-law got Alf Stevenson a job with the United Grain Growers elevator, but was not happy about two months after the marriage, when, as the widow put it, she and Alf Stevenson had not even entered a major period of adjustment, and Alf Stevenson was blown to Kingdom Come, making the former Beatrice Ann Birkland a widow.

Blown to Kingdom Come, I was led to believe, had something to do with spontaneous combustion, a concept I had trouble with until Daddy staged a practical demonstration. Daddy took a couple of oil-and-grease-soaked rags from the machine shed, balled them up real tight and put them on top of two pieces of scrap lumber on the ground in the middle of the yard. He piled a few more pieces of scrap lumber on top of the rags, and left the whole mess to sit in the sun for about forty-eight hours. When Daddy uncovered the oil-and-grease-soaked rags I was duly impressed by the temperature of the rags. Daddy then explained that tons of grain piled on itself gets hotter than a few oil-and-grease-soaked rags, and ignites itself by what is called spontaneous combustion, which the United Grain Growers elevator, known to one and all as UGG, did, blowing the newly married Alf Stevenson to Kingdom Come and creating a widow whose widowhood had lasted for fifteen years.

The widow, once she recovered from the initial shock of her brand new husband being blown to Kingdom Come, became somewhat happier to discover that the United Grain Growers elevator employee death-benefit package entitled her to a lifetime pension which, as she put it, while not allowing her to live extravagantly, certainly provided the necessities. The United Grain Growers elevator or its insurers or possibly both altered the death-benefits package shortly after Alf Stevenson was blown to Kingdom Come to make sure that future widows weren't entitled to pensions until they reached sixty-five years of age without remarrying, which cut their claims by about 100 per cent.

The wedding was to take place at the Christ on the Cross Scandinavian Lutheran Church in New Oslo, the Reverend Ibsen officiating, and there was a certain amount of restoration needed to both the church and the reverend before either one was suitable for the ceremony. The Christ on the Cross Scandinavian Lutheran Church had been in a steady state of decline ever since 1929, when the stock market crashed and banker Olaf Gordonjensen, the founder, discovered that he, like almost everyone else in North America, was more or less insolvent. The first thing that got cut was the Reverend Ibsen's salary and the second thing was repairs and maintenance to the church.

The Reverend Ibsen eventually had to rent a quarter-section of worthless land, but his total income from the farm, which was generally a minus figure, still exceeded his income from the Christ on the Cross Scandinavian Lutheran Church. The people who attended the Christ on the Cross Scandinavian Lutheran Church generally had done so at the urging of banker Olaf Gordonjensen, the banker being inclined to reduce interest rates on loans 1/4 per cent for those who attended church regularly and took heed of Reverend Ibsen's sermons dealing with the everlasting hell awaiting people who did not pay their loan instalments on time.

The 1/4 per cent banker Olaf Gordonjensen discounted was then donated to the Christ on the Cross Scandinavian Lutheran Church, until the Depression arrived and everyone found themselves more or less insolvent and unable to make loan payments even if everlasting hell awaited them.

Banker Gordonjensen eventually died, more from a ruptured wallet than anything physical, Daddy said, and debtors were released from their obligation to attend church, which caused weekly attendance to fall about 80 per cent. The remaining 20 per cent, who attended out of religious feelings rather than financial obligation, were, like everyone else, more or less insolvent, and felt guilty about listening to the Reverend Ibsen's sermons and taking up the Reverend Ibsen's time while being unable to contribute to his upkeep, and gradually drifted away, the church and the Reverend Ibsen simultaneously falling into a state of advanced disrepair.

Making repairs to a church was something that everybody in the Six Towns Area could relate to.

"We are not a people who deal in nebulous matters," the widow, Mrs. Beatrice Ann Stevenson, said to my mama one afternoon while they were having tea in our kitchen, the widow being the only one in the Six Towns Area who had gone to college, even if it was only the high-school part of the Camrose Lutheran College, and so entitled to use larger than average words.

That afternoon the widow also expressed doubts about her decision to marry Earl J. Rasmussen.

"I really have my doubts, Olivia," is how she began. "I mean our intellectual backgrounds are so different. I don't know if I can marry a man who pronounces radio as RAHD-e-o, and schedule as Sh-DOOL, and works both words into conversation several times each day."

"We all have to make allowances while working toward ultimate happiness," said Mama, in what I regarded, after I looked the word up, as *nebulous* a statement as anyone was likely to make.

"What you got to consider, Mrs. Stevenson" — Mama was not one for addressing her neighbors by their first names — "is if your life as Mrs. Earl J. Rasmussen will be significantly better than it is presently."

"For one thing, Olivia, I will never be Mrs. Earl J. Rasmussen. If Miss Quick the school teacher can be married to the infamous

Flop Skaalrud's brother and still be Miss Quick, then I can be married to Earl J. Rasmussen and still be Beatrice Ann Stevenson."

She had, the widow said, become quite attached to the name Stevenson, even though her husband Alf Stevenson had been blown to Kingdom Come before they had even emerged from a major period of adjustment, and she couldn't see any reason to disrupt her life and personal stationery by changing her name.

Mama suggested that the widow should make up her mind about the wedding quickly, for there was a Church Maintenance Bee scheduled for Sunday afternoon, weather permitting, and virtually everyone in the Six Towns Area was set to converge on the Christ on the Cross Scandinavian Lutheran Church to sweep it out, dislodge the birds' nests, wasps' nests, garter snake nests and field mouse enclaves, and paint the whole place to within an inch of its life, replace broken glass, and slap a little varnish on the pews, while a few of the older women were set to sew up a suitable outfit for the Reverend Ibsen.

"That is right nice of everybody," said the widow. Finding a bachelor in the Six Towns Area who is inclined to wash occasionally as well as being able to read and carry on a semi-intelligent conversation, even if he does say RAHD-e-o, and sh-DOOL and does shout out "Casey at the Bat" at the top of his lungs at sports days and box socials, is in many ways a blessing. Though I do consider it gauche to recite "Casey at the Bat" at an ethnic wedding.

"And it would be nice to have someone around to converse with in the evenings, and it would be a godsend to have someone to shovel a path to the outhouse in the dead of winter."

The widow took a long drink from her tea and quite daintily snipped off the edge of a home-made ginger snap, using only her front teeth and her bottom lip.

"I have told Earl J. I will marry him, and I guess there's no real reason for me to go back on my word," said the widow, sighing deeply.

"All you needed to do was talk out your worries," said Mama, snipping off the edge of a ginger snap herself.

It was surprising to find that Earl J. Rasmussen, who, for my entire lifetime, and, Daddy said, considerably beyond my lifetime, had been letting the widow know that he was smitten with her and was hers for the taking, should also have doubts about getting married.

Earl J. Rasmussen, a tall, red-faced man with golden-colored hair that curled down over his collar, was inclined, on days when he kept to his sheep-shearing sh-DOOL, to ride over to our house and drink coffee with Daddy when his work was done. Mama said, but never within Daddy's hearing, that Daddy might do better in *his* success department if *he* kept to some kind of sh-DOOL.

One day I squeezed in between the woodbox and the cook stove too late to hear Daddy's question but in time to hear Earl J.'s reply, which was, "Well, I reckon she is more interesting than the average, especially when she follows along."

"Follows along?" said Daddy.

"That woman is inclined to quote poetry at the oddest moments, if you know what I mean."

"I have heard tell that some women do that," said Daddy.

"It is downright disconcerting to be actively engaged in certain amorous activities that generally require the full attention of two parties, only to hear the other party say something like, 'Those who dream by day are cognizant of many things that escape those who dream only by night.' Or, 'I love to see it lap the miles and eat the valleys up.' Tends to take the starch out if you know what I mean."

Daddy said he knew exactly what Earl J. Rasmussen was saying, starch being of an extremely fragile nature, and he sympathized, he really did.

"Even when amorous performance is not the question, that woman is inclined to talk more than the RAHD-e-o," said Earl J. Rasmussen, "while unlike the RAHD-e-o, she expects me to listen to and comment on everything she says. I am worried that with that woman around twenty-four hours a day, I won't be able to keep to my various sh-DOOLS concerning lambing, and shearing, mating, haying, fencing, and so forth. I also worry that her constant talking will eventually drive me mad."

"Do I detect an attack of cold feet?" Daddy asked.

"I am just reassessing my situation," said Earl J. Rasmussen.

"What you got to decide," Daddy said, "is will your life being married to the widow be better than it is now, the same as it is now, or worse than it is now?"

This launched Earl J. Rasmussen into a long recitation concerning his courtship of the widow, ending with remarks to the effect that what we think we want isn't always what we really want, but we don't find out until we get what we think we want.

Daddy, to change the subject, told a few stories about his courting girls in South Carolina, which led Earl J. Rasmussen to reminisce about his courting young women in Minnesota, the only difference seeming to me to be that Daddy did his courting in a warm climate and Earl J. did his courting in cold climate. Their most interesting experiences took place in the dead of night in a wagon box while the vehicle in question was moving, being pulled by a team of horses that could find their way home by themselves.

Earl J. Rasmussen commented on how almost every girl in Minnesota who got married was pregnant when she did so, and wondered if that was a Minnesota phenomenon. Daddy said girls being pregnant when they got married was a universal phenomenon, not limited to Minnesota or South Carolina, and certainly highly prevalent in Alberta in general and the Six Towns Area in particular, though he did think it odd that no one ever mentioned the pregnancy no matter how distended the wedding gown, and pretended to be surprised by the whopping premature babies produced.

"I have always thought it would be interesting to see what size those babies would be at full term," said Earl J. Rasmussen.

Daddy slyly asked if there was any truth to the rumor that the widow was having to make some last-minute alterations to *her* wedding gown, and Earl J. Rasmussen slyly replied that the rumor was true, but not for the reason Daddy might have thought. Earl J. said that the widow, in spite of being a widow for more years than she generally cared to mention, was still in her early thirties and certainly capable of presenting Earl J. with a healthy family, which was one of her charms, as one of the things he dreamed about on his long evenings in the hills was the patter of little human feet and the banter of little human voices.

Daddy said that sounded like the best reason he had heard for going ahead with the marriage, and that he enjoyed the patter of little human feet (mine) and the banter of a little human voice (mine), and his tragedy to date had been losing his little daughter to the vagaries of life. "But what about the wedding dress?" asked Daddy.

Earl J. explained that the widow was hell-bent and determined to wear the same dress she had worn when she married Alf Stevenson, but she was no longer a teenage bride, but a thirtyish widow, who, as far as Earl J. was concerned, had filled out in all the right and proper places.

I had heard Earl J. Rasmussen claim, on any number of occasions, that a good woman should provide heat in the winter and shade in the summer. And the widow, Mrs. Beatrice Ann Stevenson, certainly filled that bill, unlike my mama, who, Daddy said, didn't have enough excess to her to pad a crutch.

"You know," Earl J. Rasmussen said, "the widow has a few qualms about the wedding herself."

"No," said Daddy, drawing the word out until it was a question.

"She has repeatedly stated to me and, if I understand right, to almost everyone else in the Six Towns Area, that she is uncertain whether she can establish domestic tranquility with a man who owns about six hundred sheep and is inclined to recite 'Casey at the Bat' in a clear and resonant voice at every box social, barn dance, whist drive, sports day, or ethnic wedding in the Six Towns Area."

"I believe she's also mentioned the fact that you've been known to comb a little axle grease into that cinnamon-colored hair of yours."

"Eau de Grease Gun," said Earl J. Rasmussen, fingering the crow's-tail cowlick at the back of his head. "I reckon I could lay off the axle grease. Tends to play havoc with the widow's sofa cushions, not to mention her pillow slips." And Earl J. Rasmussen grinned slyly.

"The course of true love never runs smooth," said Daddy, a statement that particularly impressed me.

I took a short break from listening to purloin a peanut-butter cookie or two from the pantry off the kitchen, and returned too late to hear Earl J. Rasmussen's question, but not too late to hear Daddy's answer.

"I'm inclined to believe that following along more than 50 per cent of the time is about the most you can expect," said Daddy. There are exceptions, of course," and it was Daddy's turn to smile slyly.

"Well, Johnny, never having spent nearly ten years exclusively in the company of about six hundred sheep, you can't have any idea what that experience is like, but analyzing the choices you gave me, I have come to the conclusion that the quality of my life with the widow, even if she continues to want to be called Beatrice Ann Stevenson, can't help but be better than it is now."

"All you needed to do was talk out your fears," said Daddy, and refilled their cups from the gray enamel coffee pot that lived on the back of the cook stove, smiling like he had just swallowed a canary.

Chapter Eleven

The bachelor party for Earl J. Rasmussen was held in our seldom-used living room and our often-used kitchen in our big old house at the end of Nine Pin Road. After about the fifth round of dandelion wine, chokecherry wine, raisin wine, homemade beer, and good old heathen's rapture, bring-on-blindness, logging-boot-to-the-side-of-the-head home brew, groom-to-be Earl J. Rasmussen suggested to Sven Bjornsen of the Bjornsen Bros. Swinging Cowboy Musicmakers that they should play a musical tribute to sheep. When the suggestion failed to draw any immediate reaction from the Swinging Cowboy Musicmakers, Earl J. suggested "How Great Thou Art" might be an appropriate place to start.

Daddy allowed as how he couldn't recall there being any songs written specifically about sheep.

"If that's true," said Earl J., "it's a terrible oversight, and a definite slight to the finest four-footed critters I have ever had the pleasure of knowing."

Bandy Wicker interrupted to say that in certain Texas counties it is illegal for a bachelor to own sheep, and that that is probably not a bad law.

"With the exception of a few hymns," Daddy went on as if he hadn't been interrupted, "where the sheep are not really sheep, but metaphorical sheep."

"I understand they got some veterinary medicine can cure sheep of being metaphorical," said Bandy Wicker.

"Although," Daddy said, "'Bringing in the Sheaves' is one hymn I assume has been misprinted from time immemorial and was meant to be 'Bringing in the Sheep.'"

Sven Bjornsen tapped his boot and scraped his bow across his fiddle strings and, miracle of miracles, out came "Bringing in the Sheaves," or "Bringing in the Sheep," and each member of the Bjornsen Bros. Swinging Cowboy Musicmakers joined in, and most everyone burst into song, if not with talent then with gusto.

After about eight times through they wound down, and Earl J. Rasmussen wiped tears from his eyes and thanked everyone for participating in his bachelor party. Bandy Wicker said the group had sounded almost as good as coyotes baying on a bare hilltop on a full-moon night, and that poetic language brought more tears to the eyes of Earl J. Rasmussen.

As a bachelor party present, the men of the Six Towns Area arranged for Bear Lundquist to supply the use of his inherited 1941 Pontiac Silverstreak, one of only three operational motor vehicles in the Six Towns Area, for the honeymoon.

The inherited 1941 Pontiac Silver Streak would be driven or, if the roads were bad, driven and towed, to the Edmonton–Jasper Highway containing Earl J. Rasmussen and the widow, Mrs. Beatrice Ann Stevenson, who by that time would be man and wife, bride and groom, and, as Daddy said, forever entangled in any number of ways.

The gift elicited more tears from Earl J. Rasmussen, who was feeling more mellow than most, having, Daddy said, consumed his weight plus about a quart in dandelion wine, chokecherry wine, raisin wine, homemade beer, and good old heathen's rapture, bring-on-blindness, logging-boot-to-the-side-of-the-head home brew.

Earl J. Rasmussen had a little trouble finding someone in the group to look after, herd, feed, keep tabs on, babysit, minister to, nurse, succor and serve all his about six hundred sheep while he and the widow were on their honeymoon. Babysitting six hundred sheep was not a proposition that appealed to many, and everyone in the Six Towns Area suddenly developed haying, fencing, well-digging, painting, and other urgent business.

"There is something unmanly about sheep," Bandy Wicker said, but not loud enough for Earl J. Rasmussen to hear, and Daddy and virtually everyone else in the room nodded in agreement.

Of course, it was Daddy, who being good-hearted, gullible, and a sucker for a sad story, eventually volunteered. I won't go into my experiences as a shepherd boy, or Daddy's experiences as he fed, herded, ministered to, succored and served Earl J. Rasmussen's six hundred terminally stupid sheep, except to say that over a period of fourteen days I came to the conclusion that there is indeed something unmanly about sheep.

It was shortly after the bachelor party and after the bridal shower, which took place the same night, that what became known as the Great Disappointment set in.

What precipitated the Great Disappointment was that relatives of the widow, Mrs. Beatrice Ann Stevenson, to wit one mother and seven sisters, a dozen aunts and uncles, the husbands of the seven sisters, and a whole passel of nieces and nephews, collectively decided that if their daughter, sister, sister-in-law, niece, and aunty was going to get married for a second time, they wanted it to be done in style, and since they all lived in or in the vicinity of Camrose, Alberta, the collective Birklands didn't even imagine that anywhere else but in Camrose, Alberta, could a wedding be conducted in style.

There was a last-minute flurry of correspondence which ended with a long-distance telephone call during which the collective Birkland family, who were paying for the call, played their ace — the widow would be cut out of a sizable inheritance if she didn't agree to spend the second-happiest day of her life in the company of her loved ones.

The Great Disappointment would be recalled in the Six Towns Area for years to come, for it came *after* the Church Maintenance Bee had been held and The Christ on the Cross Scandinavian Lutheran Church had been cleaned, scrubbed, and had the birds' nests, wasps' nests and colonies of mice dislodged, a few pieces of glass put back in the windows, a coat of varnish splashed on the pews, and the front step reinforced, the Great Disappointment came after the women of the Six Towns Area created a new suit for Pastor Ibsen so he would be presentable to tie the knot between the happy couple.

Mrs. Edytha Rasmussen Bozniak, no kin to Earl J. Rasmussen, rode the eastbound Western Trailways bus to Edmonton of a Tuesday morning, where in a thrift store operated by the Salvation Army, for the expenditure of only sixty-five cents, she found a blue serge suit that looked brand new.

Mrs. Edytha Rasmussen Bozniak explained that the blue serge suit was several sizes larger than the Rev. Ibsen, so it could easily be cut to specifications. The Rev. Ibsen's wife was instructed to take the intimate measurements of the Rev. Ibsen and pass the intimate measurements on to the Fark Sewing Circle and Temperance Society, who, of a Thursday afternoon at Mrs. Wasyl Lakusta's, sliced up that blue serge suit like they were dicing lettuce for a salad and reassembled it to fit the exact intimate measurements of the Rev. Ibsen.

So with both the Christ on the Cross Scandinavian Lutheran Church and the Rev. Ibsen spruced up to within an inch of their lives, the residents of the Six Towns Area were all set to celebrate the marriage of two of their own, a marriage that while it did take place did not take place in the Six Towns Area, but in Camrose, at the Christ Is King Scandinavian Lutheran Church on 51st Avenue, before the elderly Rev. Einar Solvang, who had married Beatrice Ann Birkland's parents and baptized Beatrice Ann Birkland and married Beatrice Ann Birkland and the soon to be spontaneously combusted Alf Stevenson.

"It's a good thing we already held the bachelor party and the bridal shower," Mrs. Edytha Rasmussen Bozniak said, when she found out the wedding was not going to be held at the Christ on the Cross Scandinavian Lutheran Church after all. She then suggested that a poll be taken to see if there should be a recall of the shower gifts or a moratorium declared on all wedding gifts for the happy couple who, Mrs. Edytha Rasmussen Bozniak trumpeted, were deserting the Six Towns Area.

The residents of the Six Towns Area, though they understood the pressures put on the widow by her large family, felt betrayed by her going off to Camrose, to, as the widow so aptly phrased it, "enjoy my second nuptials, and the second-happiest day of my life, in the all-encompassing bosom of my family," even though the all-encompassing bosom of her family had blackmailed her into moving the wedding.

There was an emergency meeting of the Farmers Union of Alberta, New Oslo Chapter #14, held in the seldom-used living room of our big old house at the end of Nine Pin Road, where by a vote of six to five, my daddy casting the deciding vote, it was decided not to revoke the collective community wedding present.

On the weekend of the nuptials, the weather was sunny and dry. "It is a blessing when summer comes on a weekend and not on, say, a Tuesday and Wednesday," Daddy said.

Daddy and I accompanied Bear Lundquist in his inherited 1941 Pontiac Silverstreak to pick up the soon-to-be bride, the widow, Mrs. Beatrice Ann Stevenson, at her home.

"I didn't know she was moving permanently to Camrose," said Bear Lundquist as we pulled into the yard and saw the pile of luggage, boxes, bags, cartons, crates, and cases stacked on the front porch, down the steps, and along the flagstone side-walk banked with whitewashed rocks the size of your average fifteen-pound turkey.

"Where do you reckon we're gonna put all that stuff?" said Mrs. Bear Lundquist, who had voted to withdraw the offer of the inherited 1941 Pontiac (the women, being slightly less chari-table and more offended by the widow's defection, had voted five to one in favor of reclaiming the present).

Mrs. Bear Lundquist had a good point concerning exactly where in the inherited 1941 Pontiac Silverstreak the worldly goods of the widow, Mrs. Beatrice Ann Stevenson, were going to ride. Her and Mr. Bear Lundquist took up all the front seat, and once the widow got in the back seat with Daddy and me, there would be only the trunk to hold all the luggage, which I counted at twenty-six items, not to mention Earl J. Rasmussen, who we planned to pick up next.

Bear Lundquist unwound his arthritic body from the inher-ited 1941 Pontiac Silverstreak and opened the trunk, which for-tunately was about as big as our cellar, where, when it flooded every spring, Mama's sealers of canned chicken, vegetables, and beet pickles would bob about like otters, occasionally knocking on the cellar door in the dead of night.

I watched in awe as the trunk swallowed up about two-thirds of the containers, which meant that me and Daddy only had to hold a few cartons each on our laps, and Mrs. Bear Lundquist only had to hold a couple of large paper bags, one of which con-tained the wedding dress the widow, Mrs. Beatrice Ann Stevenson, had worn as a teenage bride when she married the soon to be annihilated by spontaneous combustion Alf Stevenson.

We traveled another eleven miles to a prearranged meeting with Earl J. Rasmussen. There wasn't even a trail to the hills where Earl J. lived alone with about six hundred sheep, so he had walked out to the edge of an aspen grove.

Fortunately, Earl J. Rasmussen traveled light. He was already wearing his only suit. Daddy remarked that the smell of mothballs would certainly keep the mosquitoes and black flies away, and Bear Lundquist wondered aloud how many moths you had to kill to get mothball odor that strong. Earl J. was wearing his only tie, his only white shirt, his only pair of black dress shoes, and the diamond socks his fiancée, the widow, had knitted for him.

I had to sit on the floor between Daddy's knees to make room for Earl J. Rasmussen as we drove another eleven miles to the Edmonton–Jasper Highway with the windows open to counteract the mothball odor, where Bear Lundquist parked the Pontiac Silverstreak on the shoulder of the gravel road and where Bear Lundquist kissed the bride and reluctantly wished her well and where Mrs. Lundquist kissed the groom and reluctantly wished him well and where Daddy kissed the bride and genuinely wished her well and shook hands with Earl J. Rasmussen and slapped him on the shoulder with genuine feeling, and where the widow, Mrs. Beatrice Ann Stevenson, kissed me, even though I hid most of myself behind Daddy to avoid it.

Earl J. Rasmussen then got behind the wheel of the inherited 1941 Pontiac Silverstreak and he and the widow disappeared in a grinding of gears and gravel and a cloud of pale yellowish dust, on their way, Daddy said, to their romantic destiny.

The four of us stood on the side of the Edmonton–Jasper Highway for about two hours until Bear Lundquist's son, Ole, arrived in a wagon pulled by his team of bays, and we all climbed in and began the long drive toward our widely separated homes.

With the soon to be bride and groom gone, what forever became known as The Great Disappointment truly set in. What Mrs. Edytha Rasmussen Bozniak had described as "The gala wedding of all time, the social event of the decade in the Six Towns Area," had fizzled down to the four of us seeing the bride and groom off, standing on the edge of the Edmonton–Jasper Highway near Bjornsen's Corner and waving into a plume of yellowish dust and a grinding of gears and gravel.

We were barely out of bed the next morning, and Mama was just frying eggs and boiling grits, when a horse and cart pulled into our yard, the horse being named Lutefisk and the cart containing Mrs. Irma Rasmussen, her daughter Mrs. Edytha Rasmussen Bozniak, and her granddaughter Velvet Rasmussen Bozniak. I liked my grits boiled with a little milk and sugar on them. Daddy liked his boiled, then fried and served with a big pat of butter leaning lopsided as it melted in about three directions at once.

"Grits," Daddy said, "sort of peter out about St. Louis, Missouri. Anywhere north of St. Louis, you either have to suffer silently or acquire your grits by mail order."

Daddy couldn't afford to acquire grits by mail order, but about two or three times a year, one of Daddy's sisters, I think they took turns, sent us a twenty-five-pound bag of grits wrapped in about an equal weight of religious tracts and with little tin religious medals falling every which way when the package was opened.

"My sisters figure that the way to man's heart and soul is through his stomach," Daddy said, stuffing the religious tracts and medals into the ruby red mouth of the cookstove while eying the bag of grits which originated at the Robert E. Lee Flour Mill of Darlington, South Carolina, and licking his lips.

Mrs. Edytha Rasmussen Bozniak was practically dancing about our kitchen as she and her mama and daughter took off their jackets and settled in to the coffee Mama was pouring from the gray enamel coffee pot that lived on the back of the cook stove.

"I reckon we have to learn to take The Great Disappointment in stride," was the way Mrs. Edytha Rasmussen Bozniak opened.

Mama said she supposed that was true, and Lord knows Mrs. Edytha Rasmussen Bozniak had had her share of life's great disappointments to contend with, losing her full-scholarshipped, orphaned genius of a husband, Arthur Bozniak, as one of the first casualties of World War Two, and having to raise a daughter all by herself in a mightily depressed economy. Daddy winked at me sort of to say that even if we all knew what Mama said was not exactly the truth, we all had the good manners not to mention the truth around Mrs. Edytha Rasmussen Bozniak or any of her family.

With the social amenities out of the way, Mrs. Edytha Rasmussen Bozniak got down to business concerning the return of the newlyweds to the Six Towns Area. We had to make an effort to no longer refer to Mrs. Beatrice Ann Stevenson as "the widow" since that would surely make the new groom, Earl J. Rasmussen, uncomfortable, and we had to make every effort to conform with Mrs. Beatrice Ann Stevenson's wishes that she continue to be called Mrs. Beatrice Ann Stevenson, even if in the eyes of the Lord she was good and truly married to Earl J. Rasmussen, and even if there was something unspeakable, unnatural, and totally inappropriate about a woman not taking her husband's name as part of the nuptials, and she had been proud to become Mrs. Arthur Bozniak on the day she had married her full-scholarshipped orphaned genius who was shortly to be taken away from her by the ravages of war.

During that speech Daddy winked at me again, to say that if what Mrs. Edytha Rasmussen Bozniak was saying wasn't exactly the truth, it was close enough for us to keep our mouths shut.

Velvet Bozniak grinned at me with her smile that not only said, I know something you don't know, but also I know a whole passel of things you don't know, and stroked her Shirley Temple doll in a manner that could be considered salacious if not downright obscene.

"We were busy making social calls all day yesterday," Mrs Edytha Rasmussen Bozniak said specifically to Mama, "and it is a fact that in spite of The Great Disappointment, the majority of the women in the Six Towns Area, of whom I hope we can count you as one, have decided grudgingly to make the best of a bad situation and forgive the widow for defecting to Camrose and for submitting to the blackmail of her tribe by moving the wedding."

"I don't rightly care one way or another," Mama said.

But Mrs. Edytha Rasmussen Bozniak wanted to be sure that the situation was properly explained and itemized. "Can you imagine," she said, "how I would feel if my darling Velvet, when she gets a little older, was living away from home and decided to celebrate her wedding nuptials anywhere but right here in the Six Towns Area at the Christ on the Cross Scandinavian Lutheran Church with the Rev. Ibsen officiating? I'm certain you'd feel the same if your darling Jamie there, when he's a little older of course, decided to hold his nuptials anywhere but right here in the Six Towns Area."

"I hope," said Mama, "by the time Jamie is ready to choose a bride, that both he and we are far away from the Six Towns Area, and I don't know as I'd care where Jamie chose to get married, so long as he chose a pleasant girl to marry and was happy with the choice he had made."

"Well," huffed Mrs. Edytha Rasmussen Bozniak, and I could see the gears turning in her head and her deciding that her purpose was too important to be disrupted by a disagreement over a strictly hypothetical situation. "What we propose is that the Saturday night after the happy couple returns to the Six Towns

Area, we stage a re-enactment of the wedding. Weather permitting, the Bear Lundquists will pick up the bride and groom in style, in the Lundquists' 1941 Pontiac Silverstreak, which its very self will be a reminder of their nuptials and honeymoon. The bride and groom will dress in their wedding finery, and the Lundquists will transport them to the Christ on the Cross Scandinavian Lutheran Church, where the majority of the residents of the Six Towns Area will be sitting in the pews. The Bjornsen Bros. Swinging Cowboy Musicmakers will play 'Here Comes The Bride,' just like they would have done if the wedding hadn't been literally stolen from under our noses by the bride's nasty and possessive family, and the bride will sashay down the aisle, and the Rev. Ibsen will simulate the service, without actually performing a certifiable wedding.

"There will be a reception, a dance, a send off, possibly a chivaree, and this wedding will be a gala event of the season and possibly the social event of the decade, and after it's over we will all pretend The Great Disappointment never happened."

Daddy said he couldn't quite get his imagination around the widow, Mrs. Beatrice Ann Stevenson, sashaying, but otherwise the plan seemed inspired.

Mrs. Edytha Rasmussen Bozniak, feeling truly conciliatory, said that some of the less socially aware brides in the Six Towns Area might sashay, but the widow, Mrs. Beatrice Ann Stevenson, would probably move regally down the aisle.

Mama, who was also feeling conciliatory, blaming her sharp tongue on the fact she hadn't had her breakfast yet, said that she also felt that Mrs. Edytha Rasmussen Bozniak's plan was inspired.

Velvet Rasmussen Bozniak continued to stroke her Shirley Temple doll in a way I knew she would later suggest, if I couldn't keep us from being alone, that I should stroke her or she should stroke me.

Fortunately, the Rasmussen clan decided to move on and make some further house calls, so I was spared the advances of Velvet Rasmussen Bozniak, and spared having to dangle Velvet's Shirley Temple doll over the firebox of the cook stove in order to get her mind off the things she claimed built a baby.

As the plans for the project advanced, Mrs. Edytha Rasmussen Bozniak stuck to her guns. As a means of atonement to the women of the Six Towns Area who had grudgingly forgiven her, the widow was to wear her full wedding regalia to both church and wedding dance, though there was some division of opinion as to whether she should wear her wedding dress if there was a chivaree.

The men of the Six Towns Area didn't care what Earl J. Rasmussen wore, but with sometimes considerably more than a little pressure from the women of the Six Towns Area, the men mentioned casually to Earl J. Rasmussen that he would make their lives a lot calmer if he wore his only suit to the mock wedding and the party afterwards, along with his only tie, a hand-painted one with green palm trees on an aquamarine background featuring a hula girl swiveling her hips on a sandy beach.

Earl J. Rasmussen was, as Daddy said, still slightly euphoric from the splendor of his wedding and honeymoon and the joy of being reunited with his six hundred sheep, when he said he would be happy to oblige his friends' simple request to dress up for the re-enactment of his wedding and the party afterwards.

The community told Earl J. Rasmussen and his bride that the event began at 8:00 P.M., but everyone else in the community was instructed to be present at the Christ on the Cross Scandinavian Lutheran Church by 7:30 P.M., or they wouldn't be admitted. By the time Earl J. Rasmussen and his bride arrived at 7:45 P.M., everyone else in the Six Towns Area was already there, dressed to the nines and spoiling with excitement.

The Bjornsen Bros. Swinging Cowboy Musicmakers, the collars of their red-clover-and-white plaid shirts buttoned at the neck, each one wearing a string tie held by a genuine brass Texas armadillo, broke into an up-tempo rendition of "Here Comes the Bride," at the appropriate moment, after warming up the audience with a few Jimmy Rodgers train songs, "The Wreck of the Old 97" being a particular favorite.

The Bjornsen who played the piano pumped away on the organ, which Daddy said appeared to have lung trouble, possibly because a nest of sparrows was lodged somewheres in its insides.

During the up-tempo rendition of "Here Comes the Bride" the happy couple minus bridesmaids, flower girls, ring-bearers, groom attendants, and ushers — some things you just couldn't simulate, Mrs. Edytha Rasmussen Bozniak said — marched down the aisle to where the Rev. Ibsen, resplendent in his new-to-him suit, was waiting with an open Bible in his hand. The congregation felt free to go "ooooh" and "aaaah" at the beauty of Mrs. Beatrice Ann Stevenson, who had been dieting assiduously ever since she had accepted Earl J. Rasmussen's proposal of marriage.

There had been a certain amount of unhappiness and some downright hostility in the male community, most of it directed in the direction of Earl J. Rasmussen, because, while the widow, Mrs. Beatrice Ann Stevenson, had sisters who would be her matron of honor and bridesmaids, and nieces to be flower girls and nephews to be ring-bearers, the groom, Earl J. Rasmussen, had no close relatives, so the members of his wedding party were to have been from the Six Towns Area. Actually, Daddy was to be best man, and I was going to be ring-bearer, while Bear Lundquist and the infamous Flop Skaalrud were supposed to be ushers. But then the wedding had been stolen from under our very noses.

There was still a certain amount of unhappiness and hostility, and even a touch or two of rancor, among the male community of the Six Towns Area being directed toward Earl J. Rasmussen, Bear Lundquist feeling, for instance, and not without justification, that in payment for the use of his inherited 1941 Pontiac Silversteak, wedding present or not, he was entitled to be an usher at the mock wedding. And while Daddy didn't say so, I believe he felt that he was entitled to be best man, especially since he had spent Earl J. Rasmussen's honeymoon back in the hills babysitting Earl J. Rasmussen's six hundred sheep, in spite of his genuine feeling that there was something unmanly about sheep; and though I didn't say so, I felt I was entitled to be ringbearer at the reconstituted wedding, because I had spent a good part of Earl J.'s honeymoon back in the hills with Daddy, babysitting Earl J.'s six hundred sheep, and I too felt that there was something unmanly about sheep that I hoped would not rub off on me.

The infamous Flop Skaalrud said he was relieved not to have to be an usher at the real thing and was equally relieved at not having to be an usher at the reconstituted wedding, for the only usher he had ever seen was at the Rialto Theater in Edmonton, and he wondered if he had to buy himself a flashlight with a red hood on the end of it to be an usher at a wedding.

Daddy said in reply that the flashlight somehow reminded him of Flop Skaalrud, with Flop being quick to agree and also mentioning that being usher would allow him access to the one or two unattached women in the Six Towns Area who hadn't succumbed to his blatant male aura. So Flop Skaalrud, in spite of everything, was at least disappointed that he didn't get to be an usher.

When talking to Earl J. Rasmussen, Daddy said he understood perfectly that Earl J. Rasmussen had had nothing to do with the wedding being moved to a distant location, and that if he couldn't participate in the real thing he saw no reason to participate in a re-creation of the real thing. Daddy said that there was no point in antagonizing Earl J., for in a few weeks the whole wedding business would be forgotten.

The happy couple in full wedding regalia marched down the aisle amid a chorus of "oooos" and "aaaahs," and came face-to-face with the Rev. Ibsen, all decked out in his new-to-him suit manufactured by the women of the Six Towns Area. Rev. Ibsen cleared his throat and repeated most of the wedding vows, though the audience, most of them understanding they were watching a simulated wedding, said things aloud after each vow like "Way to go, Earl," and "You sure you want to take that varmint until death do you part, Widow Stevenson?" And "You realize you're not just gaining a husband but also six hundred sheep?" After the completion of each vow there was scattered to fulsome applause, depending on the significance of the vow to the listening audience.

When the simulated vows were over Earl J. kissed the bride, and as he did so a surprising number of cowbells emerged from under the pews and a din like nothing I had ever heard ensued for a full three minutes, increasing ten-fold each time it looked as if Earl J. Rasmussen might terminate the kiss.

When the erstwhile congregation finally quieted down, the Rev. Ibsen, as a concession to the older folks at the gathering, many of whom spoke only Norwegian and quite a few of whom weren't entirely sure what was going on, reconstituted the wedding once again in Norwegian.

As the Norwegian version unfolded, there were comments and applause from the audience; and also comments from old Ingemar Isaacson, who was seated right behind us and was, as Mama said, deaf as a stone. Ingemar Isaacson barked out something that everyone who understood Norwegian laughed at, and which Mrs. McClintock translated as, "He looks skinny as a skeleton. Does his woman know how to make lutefisk?" A moment later he said something that drew even more laughter, even from the bride and groom and Rev. Ibsen, which Mrs. Gunhilda Gordonjensen McClintock translated as "Is the bride pregnant or does she always look like that?" Someone else shouted out, "You can't stop a Norwegian wedding," and the whole congregation broke into applause.

After the ceremony had been reconstituted in Norwegian, and after the second kiss, which was live and not reconstituted at all, and also accompanied by the din of ringing cowbells and this time lasting for the better part of seven minutes, the bride and groom marched back up the aisle, Mrs. Beatrice Ann Stevenson smiling rapturously and Earl J. Rasmussen, in spite of the fact that the widow had not taken his name, grinning like he just swallowed a canary, where they prepared to shake hands with well-wishers and adjourn to the New Oslo Community Hall, where the wedding dance and party was to be held.

But the community had different ideas.

Just as the happy couple got to the back door of the Christ on the Cross Scandinavian Lutheran Church there came the sound of an alarm clock going off, and at the sound the crowd made a joyful furor, and Earl J. Rasmussen and Mrs. Beatrice Ann Stevenson, who seemed to know what was expected of them, searched around the church until they discovered the ringing clock under a pew occupied by Mr. and Mrs. Bear Lundquist, and next to the alarm clock they discovered a wedding present wrapped in blue and white paper and tied with blue ribbon in a double bow. The crowd continued to create a joyful furor until the wedding present was unwrapped and the embroidered pillow slip displayed and until Earl J. Rasmussen kissed the bride, at which point all the cowbells appeared from under the pews and the joyful furor became outright clamor.

The happy couple then turned toward the door, but just as they did so another alarm clock went off, and at that point I realized why it was that Mama had placed our old yellow Westclox alarm clock in her handbag as we were leaving the farm that afternoon. Our clock had most of its enamel worn off from being handled so much, and Mama had scratched the date of purchase on the bottom of the clock, Oct. 1, 1937, which meant that the clock was not much younger than I was, and I remembered one October when it was snowing, as it was inclined to do in Alberta in October, and not having much to do, I insisted on having a birthday party for the yellow Westclox clock, which we did, Mama baking a single cupcake and cramming six candles on it, and allowing my cowardly dog Benito Mussolini to sit across from me at a card table while I sang happy birthday to the yellow Westclox alarm clock.

Tracking down the second clock, the newlyweds found a present from Slow Andy McMahon, the Fark storekeeper, a four-pound pail of Aylmer's Strawberry Jam, "No Pectin Added." After they displayed the jam for everybody to see, the cowbells appeared again and rattled until Earl J. Rasmussen gave the bride another lengthy kiss.

Daddy and Mama were about fifteenth on some prearranged list. Daddy set the old yellow Westclox alarm clock on the floor and at the proper moment pulled the alarm button and the clock burbled loud and clear. Earl J. Rasmussen and his bride followed the noise until they recovered a package wrapped in shiny navy blue paper, which turned out to hold two white bath towels, one saying "His" and one saying "Hers." The bath towels had been a present to Mama and Daddy from one of Daddy's sisters in a year when times were better than they were now.

By the time the last alarm clock had been turned off and the last present opened and displayed and the last kiss planted on the bride by Earl J. Rasmussen and the last cowbell stopped clanging, everyone was truly ready to adjourn to the New Oslo Community Hall, where the Bjornsen Bros. Swinging Cowboy Musicmakers were ready to burst into the "Red Raven Polka," a sign that an evening of dancing was about to begin.

The dance went on until about midnight, interrupted only by a lunch hour when the women of the Six Towns Area unveiled a table loaded with sandwiches, salads, and cake and during which one layer of the wedding cake was trotted out and cut into little pieces and wrapped in napkins and a piece distributed to every woman in the Six Towns Area, so they could sleep with the piece of cake under their pillow, where the piece of cake would bring happiness to those already married and a handsome beau to those who weren't.

When the dance broke up, the men, even the ones with the most energy, like my daddy and the infamous Flop Skaalrud, agreed that they were too tired to conduct a chivaree, which would have involved all of them waiting for the happy couple to get home and into bed, and then arriving at their house and standing around the yard banging on pots and pans and ringing cowbells and maybe alarm clocks until the happy couple invited everybody inside for coffee and cake.

As a finale to the evening, Mrs. Rose Lakusta's father was helped onto the stage and seated on a folding chair, where he sang a wedding song, *a capella*, in Ukrainian, wishing the bride and groom many children, a good wheat crop, a thatched roof that didn't leak, and that their cattle shouldn't get hoof and mouth disease.

To end the evening on a proper note, outside New Oslo Community Hall the Dwerynchuck twins, Wasyl and Bodhan, engaged in their customary fist fight, precipitated by a disagreement, a shoving match, and a general altercation, the subject being who had won the majority of their previous fist fights. The contest also allowed everyone in the Six Towns Area to tell Wasyl from Bodhan for the better part of a minute, for one Dwerynchuck twin landed a vicious right to the other's bridgework and an incisor bounced off the wall of New Oslo Community Hall and landed in the couch grass.

"Hey, which one are you?" somebody yelled to the Dwerynchuck minus a tooth.

"Wasyl," he replied, whereupon everyone, being able to tell one Dwerynchuck from the other, chose sides, and a few bets were placed, until less than a minute later Wasyl landed a vicious left and one of Bohdan's incisors bounced off Torval Imsdahl's shoulder and landed in the couch grass.

SECTION FOUR

The Summer Jamie Damn Near Drowned

Chapter Twelve

The summer Jamie damn near drowned came right on the heels of the winter Helen dropped by, the same summer White Chaps murdered his wife. The summer Jamie damn near drowned was not a summer at all, but a spring. Summer started on June 2lst, the longest day of the year, while the day I damn near drowned was barely in May, and the snow had only melted a few weeks before, and the ice had barely gone out of Jamie O'Day Creek, which had almost finished its annual flood.

Within a week of the water beginning to recede, Jamie O'Day Creek flowed within its banks, a glittering sun slurping up the water from the fields and sloughs and what passed for a road. The farm yard dried up and grateful hens lazed in the sunshine, spreading first one wing, then the other, taking elaborate dust baths after a long winter in the evil-smelling hen house, their pale combs soaking up sunshine, turning from the color of iodine to a ruby red, as the hens, as if ravenous for color after the bleak winter, fed on the yellow-blond heads of dandelions.

Almost before I realized it I was able to put away my gumboots and put on my sneakers.

Spring was my favorite time of year. I collected bits of tree bark from the wood box and snaffled whatever kindling I could lay my hands on without Mama getting too cross, and I cut paper sails out of the glossy pages of the mail-order catalogue, or wish book as Daddy called it. The sails were large, medium, and small triangles of color, which I attached with varying degrees of craftsmanship to the bits of tree bark and pieces of kindling.

One dazzling afternoon, when the sky was high and blue as cornflowers, I placed a dozen boats in a small cardboard box that had once contained cans of Aylmer's tomato soup, and with my cowardly dog Benito Mussolini tagging along well behind, in case I encountered anything dangerous, I set off to sail my toys in Jamie O'Day Creek.

About a half-mile from our house, I chose a spot the afternoon sun shone on constantly, a spot where the new grass was already soft and measled with dandelions, where the air smelled of budding leaves, open flowers, and clean water. I picked a golden dandelion and placed it on my tongue, chewing it slowly, savoring the bitter green taste, for, stepping out of the months-long black-and-white movie of winter, I too was starved for color.

I loved the clear, cold water close up. Just below the soft slope of the bank, Jamie O'Day Creek raced along, the long brown grass of last fall just below the water line, flowing like a woman's hair in a strong wind, the water tinged the color of stained oak. Since I wasn't able to swim Mama didn't like me playing around the water, so I had chosen a very safe spot as a boat-launching site.

As I played, I made up stories about the boats, where they were from and where they were going, and as each story concluded I'd lean far out over the water and let the current carry the boat away. Sometimes the boat would travel to the center of the stream and be swept down and out of sight in the direction of Purgatory Lake and the Pembina River, and, Daddy said, eventually Hudson Bay. Sometimes the boat would snag on the grasses near to shore and be tugged under by the current, the force of the water often separating the boat from the sail.

Most of the boats tipped over quickly, but one with a red sail composed mainly of a scarlet dress from the women's-wear section of the mail-order catalogue attached to a wafer-thin piece of kindling skimmed along the top of the bubbling water, the sun reflecting off the glossy paper of the sail. I watched that boat until it was almost out of sight, disappearing in the direction of Purgatory Lake, the Pembina River, and possibly Hudson Bay.

It was because of a boat that got caught in the long, tress-like grasses along the creek bank that the accident happened. I moved several feet along the bank and decided that with a long, careful stretch I could recover the boat from the underwater grasses, repair the sail, and launch it again. I really thought I could complete the rescue without endangering myself or I wouldn't have attempted it. I was stretching as far as I could and was within an inch or two of recovering the boat when I started to slide. Before I knew it I was in the clear, cold water of Jamie O'Day Creek. Then I was under the water of Jamie O'Day Creek.

Within seconds my clothes felt as if they weighed a hundred pounds. I wasn't terribly scared, and my life didn't flash before my eyes. I kept thinking it was all a mistake and I'd soon be able to reach the bank and pull myself out of the water. I continued to think that, until, just like my boat with the red sail, I was pulled into the current and swept away downstream toward Purgatory Lake, the Pembina River, and possibly Hudson Bay.

I remember considering the possibility that Benito Mussolini would rescue me, and for an instant saw a picture on the front page of the *Sangudo Semi-Monthly,* me with my arm around

Benito Mussolini, him licking my face, under a headline: HEROIC
DOG RESCUES MASTER FROM DROWNING.

I suppose that fantasy was somewhat similar to having my
life flash before my eyes, for even as I was drowning I remembered that my cowardly dog Benito Mussolini was even more
terrified of water than I was. I did recall a picture of Benito
Mussolini, all four legs stiff as if they'd been welded, standing
forlorn and helpless on Daddy's raft, dry-heaving. So I suppose
at least part of my life did flash before my eyes.

At one point I grabbed a handful of grass on the bank, but
instead of feeling like a woman's hair, that grass was as slippery
as if it had been buttered, and slipped through my fingers as the
current carried me toward the center of the stream.

I remember thinking Mama would be really cross with me for
getting my clothes wet and muddy, that her eyes would turn
from cornflower blue to bachelor-button blue, and that her
voice would certainly twang the cutlery. Then I remember thinking it would be awful hard on Mama to lose both me and my
almost-sister Rosemary within a single year, and I pictured
Daddy and his sad, uncomfortable friends standing around my
grave. Then, instead of being cold, I was warm and comfortable, and it flashed through my mind that dying wasn't all that
bad, and I didn't remember anything else until I woke up.

The sky was the first thing I saw. I could tell by its tone and
texture that darkness was falling. I was still outdoors. A fire
flickered nearby. I was wrapped in something heavy and warm.
I closed my eyes for a second. I could smell the dying warmth of
the grass on the creek bank, the heavy perfume of leather, the
sharp odor of wood smoke. My throat felt as if I'd swallowed a
rasp. When I opened my eyes again, there was a familiar face
staring down at me.

"Helen," I said. "What are you doing here?"

Helen didn't speak, but she leaned down and hugged me to

her for a long time. I was wrapped in a horsehide robe, and Helen was drying my clothes over a campfire.

We were about two hundred yards downstream and around a gooseneck bend in Jamie O'Day Creek from where I'd fallen in. Helen must have seen me floating by and reeled me in like a fish.

I coughed for a while, my head ached and my nose and throat felt raw. I reached out and took Helen's sturdy brown hand in both of mine and held on very tight. Helen had tears in her eyes, and I reckon I had tears in mine, too.

"I am plumb glad to see you," I said, and reached up my arms to hug her again. Helen sniffled in my ear and rubbed her nose on the sleeve of the worn corduroy jacket she was wearing. She smelled of campfires, tree sap, and wildflowers.

There were so many things I wanted to ask Helen, like what was she doing camped along Jamie O'Day Creek? Where was her baby? Who was she? Did she have a name I could call her by that was really her own? Was she surprised when she saw me floating along Jamie O'Day Creek on my way toward Purgatory Lake, the Pembina River, and possibly Hudson Bay?

Some movement caught my eye and I saw a man off to the left of the campfire. He was small, though he didn't look much older than Helen, squatting on his haunches, a long-billed red cap pulled low over his face, the crown of the cap stained with sweat and dirt.

When I first looked he was staring at me. As soon as our eyes met he lowered his head, but in the instant I viewed his face I saw that his eyes were small and ferret-like, the whites yellowish, and they were filled with hate, not just for me but for the whole world.

"Mama's gonna miss me and skin me alive if I don't get home," I said to Helen, trying to get up. She smiled and indicated that that my clothes would be dry before long and gently pushed me back into the depths of the robe.

Helen shook my arm to wake me up. My clothes were dry, and Helen handed them to me piece by piece so I could dress under the horsehide robe and not get cold. I was more than a little shaky when I stood up, but Helen hugged me again, and I thanked her for saving my life and drying me out. She said a few words to me in her language. The tone was universal, for she sounded a lot like Mama when she was fussing over me and telling me I was the joy of her life and the best thing that had ever happened to her and Daddy.

I walked a few steps in the direction of home. Then I turned around and waved at Helen and smiled, and she waved back.

"Rat pie," I said.

And Helen said, "Rat pie," and we both laughed.

I never saw her again.

"Where in the world have you been?" Mama said, as I wandered into the kitchen trying to look as if nothing unusual had happened. "I was just about to come looking for you."

Then she looked more closely at me, as I sidled toward the wash basin, aiming to wash my hands and face and comb my hair so good I wouldn't draw the slightest criticism for "just moving the dirt around."

"What in the world happened to you, Jamie? You look a sight."

"I was running across the south slough," I lied, "when Benito Mussolini got tangled in my legs and I fell face first in the mud. I dried my clothes out in the sunshine for a while."

I lathered up my hands good with a green bar of Palmolive soap.

"Well, accidents happen," Mama said, smiling just a little, "but you must have about froze yourself. Your voice sounds funny. You're not catching a cold, are you?"

"I hope not," I said.

"Well, climb up here and have some soup," said Mama. "I don't know where your daddy is. Him and Earl J. Rasmussen were talking sheep out in the corral last I saw of them. I expect they're sneaking a drink in the hayloft and saying dirty words."

I wanted to tell Mama that I had fallen into Jamie O'Day Creek and that Helen had saved my life by reeling me in like a fish as I floated by on my way to Purgatory Lake, the Pembina River, and possibly Hudson Bay, and that Helen had wrapped me in a horsehide robe while she dried my clothes over a campfire, and had hugged me and made me feel real comfortable, even if she'd had a man with her who was thin as a hatchet and sat on his haunches by the campfire smoking the whole time I was recovering and my clothes were drying, looking at me with a yellow stare evil as a crow's.

But I couldn't tell Mama anything but the lies I had already told her, for if she knew I'd fallen into Jamie O'Day Creek and almost drowned, would have drowned for sure if Helen hadn't reeled me in like a fish, why Mama would never let me go alone to anywhere near Jamie O'Day Creek until I turned twenty-one, or became wealthy, or got married, whichever came first, which was most likely my turning twenty-one.

If I told Mama what really had happened, besides a conniption fit, something she threatened to have each and every time Daddy or I did something to scare or embarrass her, she would have what she called "mixed emotions," she would want to hug me and say how happy she was I was alive, and she'd want to strangle me for being so stupid and careless as to fall into Jamie O'Day Creek, especially if I told her I would have been completely dead and either tangled in last year's grasses at the bottom of Jamie O'Day Creek or floating off toward Purgatory Lake, the Pembina River, and possibly Hudson Bay, if it wasn't for Helen reeling me in like a fish.

I just ate my soup and biscuits and one oatmeal cookie without spilling or making a single crumb, and then I said I reckoned being flattened in the mud of the slough by Benito Mussolini had tired me out some, so I put my clothes in the dirty clothes box and hiked off to bed, thankful that Daddy was out in the barn with Earl J. Rasmussen, for I suspected Daddy might recognize somebody who had fallen in a creek and had their clothes dried over a campfire and was lying through their teeth about what had actually happened to them, and that was not a situation I wanted to be in.

Though I did want both Daddy and Mama to know that Helen had saved my life, and I knew both Daddy and Mama would want to reward Helen for her trouble and should reward Helen for her trouble, for once I was thankful Helen was shy and didn't speak English, otherwise she would have brought me home and explained what really happened, and I would be confined to my room until I turned twenty-one, became wealthy, or got married, whichever came first, which was likely to be my turning twenty-one.

Chapter Thirteen

It was about three months later, at the height of the summer White Chaps murdered his wife, that I confessed to Mama what had really happened the day I came home claiming to have been tripped up in the south slough by my cowardly dog Benito Mussolini.

I confessed to Mama right after an RCMP officer visited our farm at the end of Nine Pin Road. Mama and I were alone on the farm, had been alone for a month, and were likely to be alone for another month or more, for in June Daddy got a letter from a contractor in Edmonton saying the contractor had been hired by the American army to built a whole passel of Quonset huts, and all those Quonset huts needed wooden floors, and the contractor remembered that Daddy was one of the best framing carpenters he had ever seen, and offered Daddy at least two months' work at what Daddy called respectable wages building floors for Quonset huts.

Daddy, who admitted that after about his second day of

farming on our useless quarter-section of land he had had some misgivings that he hadn't stayed in Edmonton and accepted Relief and waited out the Depression in style, was on the eastbound Western Trailways bus the very next morning, carrying a change of clothes and his carpenter tools.

Daddy sent Mama money regular as clockwork, and Daddy wrote letters regular as clockwork, saying he had a nice room at the Castle Hotel on 103rd Street in Edmonton, and he generally ate breakfast at the Hollywood Inn Café, right next door to the Castle Hotel, and that the Hollywood Inn Café packed him a lunch to take to work, and he generally ate supper at the Belmont Café on 101st Street, and on Saturday nights and Sunday afternoons he generally went to Renfrew Park down on the river flats and watched some semi-professional baseball.

Daddy sent me a copy of the *St. Louis Sporting News* and a Wildfire chocolate bar in a package that was kind of a mess by the time it arrived, because the chocolate bar melted in the summer heat and obliterated a certain number of pages in the *St. Louis Sporting News*. I appreciated the gesture anyway and was thankful Daddy had taught me to read a box score, and there was a picture of two of my favorite players, Snuffy Stirnweiss and Bucky Walters, separate pictures of course, Stirnweiss was with the New York Yankees and Walters with the Cincinnati Reds.

I had never seen an RCMP officer up close before. There wasn't much call for law enforcement in the Six Towns Area, and the local mounties were stationed at Gainford, way across Purgatory Lake and the only hamlet that had a hotel. The hotel had a bar, which was why the RCMP were stationed in Gainford, because if anybody was going to make trouble in the Six Towns Area, it would be after they'd gone to the Gainford Hotel and drunk more than a few beers.

To show how much experience I'd had with the RCMP, I didn't even recognize the man who rode into our yard on a mud-splattered bay as an RCMP officer, though I knew by the felt hat he wore that he was something peculiar, but if I'd had to guess I have guessed he was a scoutmaster, for I'd seen pictures of mounties in the *Toronto Star Weekly,* and I'd seen pictures of scout-masters in the *Toronto Star Weekly,* and the fellow who rode into our yard on the mud-splattered bay looked more like a scoutmas-ter, though he looked young even for that minor responsibility.

The mounties in pictures were always dressed in scarlet uni-forms and mounted on coal-black horses shiny as polished rock, and they all had square jaws and steely eyes, and I knew if I ever met one there'd be no question about who was in charge.

That's why I was so surprised when the young fellow on the mud-splattered bay horse asked to see the lady of the house and identified himself as Constable Park of the RCMP. I thought for a minute he might be playing a joke by pretending to be a moun-tie, but I decided that even if he didn't have on the bright scarlet uniform and even if he wasn't riding a coal-black horse, shiny as polished rock, and even if he didn't have a square jaw or steely eyes, he had the seriousness necessary to be an RCMP officer, even if he hardly looked old enough to be out of high school.

I called Mama from where she was sewing in the back bed-room, where it stayed cool all year round.

The reason Constable Park was riding a mud-splattered bay was that Jamie O'Day Creek was flooding again. It had rained every day for about two weeks, long days of slanted, driving, needle-like rain, and then in the evenings, as if we hadn't suffered enough, the sky would be zippered with lightning, and thunder would rattle the window glass and bounce dishes around on the table, just like when Lorne Greene delivered the evening news on the radio in his Voice of Doom, and the sky would open and pour thousands of gallons of water directly down on us.

Though Jamie O'Day Creek wasn't flooding the fields, instead of being dried up to the width of a broom handle the way it should have been in August, it was flowing full force, almost bursting over its banks, its color yellow and surly, uprooted saplings and pieces of lumber floating rapidly along in the general direction of Purgatory Lake, the Pembina River, and possibly Hudson Bay.

The rain had stopped about two days before the young mountie made his house call, and the sun was blistering, creating a few billion mosquitoes, the smaller ones, as Daddy said, being the size of cocker spaniels, and a few billion blackflies that got in ears and eyes and noses and mouths, and got in the ears and eyes and noses and mouths of all the farm animals, too.

The first thing Mama said to Constable Park was, "Why you poor thing, you look like you been bit to a frazzle. Tie up your horse and come in for a cold drink."

Constable Park did appear as if he had been bit to a frazzle. He had dead blackflies in the corners of his mouth and eyes, he was smeared with the slapped remnants of blackflies and mosquitoes, and his face was one large mosquito bite. He had little splotches of blood where he had squashed mosquitoes that were already feeding on him.

"No thank you, Ma'am," Constable Park said. "I have to get on with my rounds. "Are you and the boy alone here?"

"Yes, we are," Mama replied. "Is there some kind of trouble?"

"We hope not, Ma'am. Have you seen any strangers? Any Indians?"

"No sir. We haven't had but two visitors in the last month, and both were neighbors. Some summers, Indians camp a mile or so south, along the road allowance, but it's been too wet this year. The saskatoon berries have been delayed by the heavy rains, and the Indians won't be around until the saskatoons ripen. But let me get you a cold drink of lemonade."

Constable Park thanked Mama and said he'd be pleased to partake of some lemonade. He didn't get down off his horse, though, he just sat there, and after Mama brought him a tall glass with sweat dripping down the outside, he took a long drink and set to explaining the purpose of his visit. He said there'd been a murder on an Indian reserve up north of Sangudo, that a young fellow named Bartholomew White Chaps had taken a rifle and killed his wife and taken a shot at his father-in-law, but missed the father-in-law, and then run off into the bush.

Constable Park said the murder had taken place going on ten days before and that they hadn't been able to find hide nor hair of White Chaps, and though they thought he had gone north, they were just checking our area in case White Chaps had come south and someone might have seen him or heard of him.

"I hate to alarm you, Ma'am," Constable Park said, "but this fellow is considered armed and dangerous, and it might be wise if you could stay with a neighbor or have a neighbor stay with you."

"I reckon we can frighten us off an Indian," Mama said. "Between me and the boy and our watch dog over there," pointing to Benito Mussolini, peeking one eye around the corner of his doghouse, where he'd gone to hide as soon as he heard the constable's horse. "If anything is out of the usual the dog will come to us for protection, which is maybe even better than if he barked and raged and let a stranger know he was here."

"I don't know," said Constable Park.

"But look at your poor face," Mama said. "Let me fix you up a little before you go on. You've got a six-mile ride to the next farm."

The constable was either unwilling or unable to get off his horse, but he let Mama give him a warm cloth to wash his face, and then he let Mama pass him a handkerchief soaked in witch hazel to ease his bitten face, and finally he let Mama pass him a bottle of citronella, which he rubbed on his face and neck and hands to keep at least some of the billion flies and mosquitoes away.

"Don't you worry about us," Mama went on. "For one thing, Indians don't come by here hardly ever, and I bet that White Chaps fellow is legging it north toward the Peace River Country right while we're talking and, besides, I've got me a .22 rifle in the back bedroom, and I can shoot the eye out of a sparrow at a hundred yards."

I knew that Mama had never shot the gun in her life, and she didn't let me touch it unless I was accompanied by Daddy, and even then she didn't like it, though Daddy used to shoot us a fine batch of Hungarian partridge and prairie chickens several times every fall and Mama used to can some of the partridge parts so we could eat meat in the dead of winter.

"You've never shot the gun in your life," was the first thing I said as soon as the constable was out of earshot.

"Well now, I didn't want him to worry. He has enough to do, what with upholding the law and fighting off the mosquitoes and blackflies. And we aren't going to go to no neighbors and end up beholden, and we aren't going to ask any neighbor to come stay with us and end up beholden. And no Indian from way up by Sangudo is going to come down this far south anyway."

"Helen did," I said.

"That was a once in a lifetime event, Jamie. Helen was lost, and she probably came from the other direction anyway."

Though she and I had never discussed the matter, I knew that Helen had come from Sangudo way, had passed Hopfstadt's farm and Deaf Danielson's place in order to get to our house at the end of Nine Pin Road. And I also had a terrible feeling when Constable Park mentioned an Indian named Bartholomew White Chaps had murdered his wife, for though I didn't know the name of the man with Helen, he looked like a White Chaps to me. I would have bet money then and there, that if Constable Park had carried a wanted poster with a picture of Bartholomew White Chaps, that's who I would have seen peering out at me.

I even think Daddy, in spite of being in the barn talking sheep with Earl J. Rasmussen and maybe sneaking a drink of good old heathen's rapture, bring-on-blindness, logging-boot-to-the-side-of-the-head home brew at the time I sidled home from Jamie O'Day Creek wearing my clothes that had just been dried over a campfire, still shaking from almost having drowned, understood that something earth-shaking had occurred. Why else would Daddy have decided the very next week that I should learn to swim? Within a few days, the water of Jamie O'Day Creek was as warm as it was ever going to get, which wasn't very warm, and the mosquitoes and black flies hadn't hatched yet.

Daddy had learned how to swim in what he called mill pools in South Carolina. I was never quite able to get a handle on what a mill pool was, though I think it might have been a fancy name for a slough, because the way Daddy described the mill pools, they sounded pretty much like sloughs to me: tepid water and lots of grass, green scum, and insects, though somehow the way Daddy told it he made tepid water and lots of grass, green scum, and insects sound pretty appealing, especially the way he recalled running down a gentle hill, and swinging from a pole he and his friends had nailed between two trees, and doing a cannonball into the mill pool.

Daddy and me didn't have no bathing suits, and even though Mama said it was positively indecent for us to swim naked, we did anyway. In spite of almost drowning in Jamie O'Day Creek I wasn't afraid of water or learning to swim, and within three days Daddy had me swimming like a fish, doing dives and rolls and bellyflops, the crab crawl, the dog paddle, and even a passable breast stroke. I figured that if I could learn to do the dog paddle then so could my cowardly dog Benito Mussolini.

Daddy picked a spot where there was a fairly sharp incline down to Jamie O'Day Creek and he took a length of baling wire and ran it between two trees, about six feet apart, and about five feet above the ground. I had to reach just over my head to grasp the wire and Daddy had to duck his knees way down to grab the wire, but we would both run down that sloped bank, grab the baling wire, and fling ourselves into Jamie O'Day Creek in a reverse cannonball.

Sometimes Daddy would pretend that he had forgot to duck his knees and that the line of baling wire had caught him right across the throat. He'd make an awful strangling sound as he flew into the water and then he'd play dead, sometimes until, even though I knew he was playing, I'd get worried and start trying to drag him out of the water. Sometimes Daddy would let me all but get him beached before he'd break into that laugh of his that was really a guffaw and could never be mistaken for anything else. Daddy could hold his breath longer than anybody I ever knew.

"You really set my nerves on edge," I'd tell him. "I about had a conniption fit."

Daddy would laugh even louder, guffawing like crazy, because I was the spitting image of my mama, he said, right down to using her language and voice inflections.

We played like that all day every day for most of a week, until Mama suggested that Daddy maybe should get interested in seeding the north field, which he promptly did.

I swam almost every day, even after the mosquitoes and blackflies hatched out, until Jamie O'Day Creek shrivelled away and became too shallow to do anything but wade in.

But now, with the unseasonable rains, I would be able to swim again, though Mama cautioned me to be careful because, she said, Jamie O'Day Creek had developed quite a current.

Chapter Fourteen

I should have known that Benito Mussolini wasn't a coward for no good reason, but as I was heading down to what I referred to in my head as the swimming hole, I noticed that Benito Mussolini got all stiff-legged and lagged way behind me and eventually disappeared completely. I guessed that there was a badger or maybe a skunk nearby, or maybe just some crows — Benito Mussolini was afraid of crows, as well as just about everything else either alive or dead.

I whipped off my clothes and went sliding down the bank to dip my toes in Jamie O'Day Creek until I got used to the water, when I caught a movement out of the corner of my eye and there, half-hidden by new aspen leaves, but recognizable all the same, was that yellowish-eyed Indian who had been with Helen when she reeled me in like a fish from Jamie O'Day Creek.

"Hi," I said, waving my left hand at him. "Is Helen with you?"

The yellowish-eyed Indian didn't speak, but stared at me in a way that let me know he hated not only me but the whole world.

"Guess Helen ain't here," I said, and in that moment I knew exactly how Benito Mussolini must feel whenever he comes close to something strange, for my thought at that moment was to place myself somewheres else just as fast as my legs would allow me.

But in the moment of eye contact with the yellowish-eyed Indian I saw something else in his eyes too. Fear. I couldn't say exactly why a yellowish-eyed Indian who could hunt and trap and live off the land would be afraid of a skinny white boy about to begin fifth grade by correspondence lessons in the fall if he lived that long, but he was. And I also knew the yellowish-eyed Indian with the hateful stare was going to do something about his fear of me.

I was right, for two seconds later, the yellowish-eyed Indian with the hateful stare was coming for me. I was happy to see he didn't have a gun, but he did have a knife sheathed on his belt, though I guess he felt his hands were all he needed to deal with a skinny white boy who might or might not get to start fifth grade by correspondence in the fall.

I scrambled up the bank of Jamie O'Day Creek, my bare toes scratching out dirt as I did so, but the yellowish-eyed Indian with the hateful stare cut at an angle through the red willow clumps, rose bushes, and aspen saplings, and cut off my retreat toward our big old house at the end of Nine Pin Road.

I was about half-way up the hill when the yellowish-eyed Indian blocked the path about twenty feet above me. He glanced down at his knife, bared his yellow teeth, and started to walk toward me.

I wondered if Indians could swim. It struck me that even though Daddy had once taken me to the reserve at Lac Ste. Anne, where we had seen hundreds of Indians on the streets and on the beach, I couldn't recall a single Indian swimming in Lac Ste. Anne.

Maybe there was safety in water. I turned and ran back down the hill, intending to grab the wire Daddy had strung between two aspen trees and catapult myself into the middle of Jamie O'Day Creek, where I figured I'd have a chance because even if the yellowish-eyed Indian dove in after me he was fully clothed and I wasn't. But as I ran I was so scared I couldn't raise my arms, and I passed under the wire and slid down the bank, and when I got to the edge I paused for one beat while I tried to decide whether to dive in or run along the bank for a ways first.

As it turned out, all I needed was that one beat. Though I just heard the contact and didn't actually see it, I'd guess the wire caught the yellowish-eyed Indian right below the chin, for when I glanced back he was heading for the water of Jamie O'Day Creek feet first, his long-billed red cap falling toward the grass of the sidehill, one hand trying to reach for his neck. The sound of wire twanging, and the half-yelp of surprise that died in the throat of the yellowish-eyed Indian rose above the gurgling sound of Jamie O'Day Creek.

The yellowish-eyed Indian hit the water with a great splash and sank like a rock. I must have counted to five or more before he reappeared in the middle of Jamie O'Day Creek, face down, the current carrying him off in the direction of Purgatory Lake, the Pembina River, and possibly Hudson Bay.

In the few seconds before the yellowish-eyed Indian disappeared around the first bend in Jamie O'Day Creek, I considered jumping in and maybe reeling him in like a fish, but then I considered that the yellowish-eyed Indian had been set to do me a certain amount of harm, and that he might be playing possum the way Daddy played possum in the water until I got worried enough to try and haul him out.

I decided not to jump in the water, and in a matter of seconds the yellowish-eyed Indian was out of sight, on his way down Jamie O'Day Creek in the direction of Purgatory Lake, the Pembina River, and quite possibly Hudson Bay. Everything was quiet again, the only sounds the gurgling of Jamie O'Day Creek and the cawing of a few crows, the only evidence that the yellowish-eyed Indian wasn't a figment of my imagination, the long-billed red cap with the grease- and sweat-stained crown, which lay on the creek bank.

I never told Mama.

She would only have felt real bad that she had endangered my life by not moving us away, even if we did become beholden to a neighbor, or having someone come to stay with us like the young, bug-bitten mountie had suggested. And Daddy, if he ever found out Mama had ignored the advice of the young bug-bitten mountie just because she didn't want to be beholden to a neighbor, would have had a conniption fit.

After I gathered up most all of my clothes I walked down the bank of Jamie O'Day Creek for a long ways, afraid of what I might find but feeling compelled to look anyways. Even though I kept my eyes open I never did spot a thing, not a twinge, not a trace, though everything did seem to get quieter than it had ever been before, even the gurgling of Jamie O'Day Creek, the cawing of an occasional crow, and the burble of a distant meadowlark seeming somehow muffled.

As soon as I stuffed myself into my clothes, and after White Chaps, or a certain yellowish-eyed Indian with a hateful stare who intended to do me harm, had drifted, face down, clean out of sight around a bend in Jamie O'Day Creek, Benito Mussolini came out from where he had been hiding in the red willow clumps and walked right beside me as we hiked down the bank, searching the current and the reeds.

Maybe White Chaps, or a certain yellowish-eyed Indian with a hateful stare who intended to do me harm, was playing a game like Daddy did when he pretended to be drowned in order to cause me to have a conniption fit. Maybe he had drifted around the bend of Jamie O'Day Creek, pulled himself from the water, and was hiking toward the Peace River Country, the way Mama believed he was all along.

After walking further down the bank of Jamie O'Day Creek than Benito Mussolini or I had ever walked before, afraid every step of what I might find, walking so far that our feet started to sink into the beginnings of a blueberry muskeg, I decided to believe the version of the White Chaps story, or the yellowish-eyed Indian story, that Mama had believed all along. I decided to believe that he had pulled himself out of Jamie O'Day Creek and was hiking toward the Peace River Country as fast as his legs could carry him. I also decided that if I believed that particular version of the White Chaps story, there was no reason for me to mention the incident to anyone, because even someone like White Chaps couldn't be in two places at once, and if he had been hiking off toward the Peace River country for several days, as Mama believed, then there was no way he could have been skulking along the banks of Jamie O'Day Creek intent on doing me harm.

I didn't know for sure, or even for partial sure, the fellow with the yellowish eyes and evil stare was White Chaps. All I knew was that he was with Helen when Helen saved my life.

I didn't know for sure, or even for partial sure, that Helen was White Chaps's wife or that White Chaps had murdered her and taken a shot at his father-in-law and was now on the run from the RCMP. All that was pure guess, and since I was the only one who had seen the yellowish-eyed Indian with the evil stare, and since the young bug-bitten mountie who visited us wasn't carrying a photo of White Chaps or a photo of Helen, and since photos of White Chaps and Helen probably didn't exist, I decided to believe Mama's version of the story.

I decided to believe that the yellowish-eyed Indian didn't

really intend to hurt me or he was just having a bad day, maybe the fish hadn't been biting and all his snares were empty, and that when he floated around the bend in Jamie O'Day Creek, good old Helen was there to reel him in like a fish, and Helen dried his clothes over the campfire while he was wrapped in a horsehide robe, and their baby was there in its little hammock, and the whole family lived happily ever after, and Helen thought of me once in a while and maybe taught her child, when it got to the right age, to say "Rat pie."

My only concession to safety came that night, just before bed time, when I sidled over from the oilcloth-covered kitchen table to the back door and I tried to slip a heavy silver table knife into the doorjamb, hoping that Mama wouldn't notice.

Mama noticed.

"What in the world are you doing, Jamie O'Day?"

"I was aiming to stick a knife in the door," I said.

"What you afraid of?"

"I guess I been thinking about what that mountie said."

"Well, if it'll make you feel better, honey, you just go right ahead, but I don't believe for a minute we have a thing to worry about. That old Indian is probably legging it toward the Peace River Country right while we're talking, that is, if the RCMP haven't arrested him by now, which I bet they have. You know the RCMP always get their man."

Somehow I couldn't equate the RCMP who always got their man with the mud-splattered, mosquito-bitten boy constable who warned us about White Chaps being on the loose and swabbed citronella on his chewed-up face before he traveled on.

What Mama said made me feel a lot better, but it was at that point, sitting across from her at the oilcloth-covered kitchen table in our big old house at the end of Nine Pin Road, both of us drinking hot chocolate Mama had just cooked up on the back burner of the stove, that I confessed I had fallen in Jamie

O'Day Creek back in May and that I would have drowned dead if Helen hadn't reeled me in like a fish from the waters of Jamie O'Day Creek.

"Why in the world didn't you tell me?" Mama said. "Looking back, I remember you acting kind of odd that day, but I never suspected such a thing. And why didn't you bring Helen back with you? Least I could have done was shook her hand and cooked her a good meal."

And while Mama sipped her hot chocolate and looked skeptical, I explained how there had been a small yellowish-eyed Indian with Helen, a man who squatted by the camp fire and stared at me like he'd enjoy killing me for no other reason than I existed.

"Oh," Mama said. "You think that man might have been White Chaps and that it might have been Helen who got murdered?"

I said I did.

Mama did her best to convince me that it was unlikely Helen was the person murdered or White Chaps was the man I'd seen with Helen on the banks of Jamie O'Day Creek, and by the time she had finished her explanation I think she had convinced herself that what she said was true.

So Mama, if she ever was scared, wasn't scared anymore and I tried to make myself believe what Mama said was true, and with the knife in the door I felt somewhat safer. We left the knife in the door every night until Daddy came home the last week of August and announced there was enough work building fine houses in Edmonton that we could move back to the city.

For days after what I referred to in my mind as The Swimming Incident, I pretended I was a mountie who always got his man, and that I was sneaking up on White Chaps's camp to arrest him. With my cowardly dog Benito Mussolini a safe distance behind me, I'd slip quietly through the woods, dodging behind bushes and trees until I was at the swimming hole, then once I was sure everything was quiet there, Benito Mussolini and I would skulk downstream until our feet began disappearing in the rubbery moss of the blueberry muskeg.

I was always afraid of what I'd find along the bank. I kept my nose open for unpleasant odors and an eye on the sky for buzzards, though Daddy assured me there were no buzzards in Alberta, and I'd have to go all the way to Utah or Arizona to find a buzzard. I never did spot a thing suspicious. After about ten forays to the muskeg, I gave up my RCMP fantasy and found easier games to play.

On one of those forays all the way to the blueberry muskeg I decided to dispose of the long-billed red cap that had belonged to the yellowish-eyed Indian, disposing with it as I did so of the last possibility of the reappearance of the yellowish-eyed Indian. I decided to dispose of the long-billed red cap in a stand of blackberry bushes a mile or so from the house. As I reached deep into the thorny mass of blackberry vines in order to dispose of the long-billed red cap I spotted something hidden there.

The winter day Helen left our farm at the end of Nine Pin Road, Daddy and I had accompanied her as far as the barn, and we had given Helen a gift I had gone to the hayloft to collect. Since Helen was expecting a baby, Daddy and I agreed she should have the crib Oslin the Estonian had carpentered for my almost-sister Rosemary.

Helen had accepted the crib, put the food and gifts Mama had given her in it and walked away, balancing it on her shoulder. But I guess Helen had only accepted the crib to be polite, and as soon as she got out of sight of our farm at the end of Nine Pin Road she decided she had no use for a crib made by Oslin the Estonian, the Lamb of God bleating picturesquely from each end. Or maybe the crib was too heavy and the walk Helen had ahead of her was too long to carry such a burden? What puzzled me was the place I'd found the crib. It was not in the direction Helen had taken when she left our farm that

December day. It was closer to the spot where Helen had reeled me in like a fish from the waters of Jamie O'Day Creek, and I've been thinking about that for all the years of my life but I've never come up with a plausible explanation.

I decided to leave well enough alone, and deposited the long-billed red cap in the now weathered white birch crib, allowing both items, as Daddy would have said, to return to their natural state.

As The Swimming Incident became more past tense than present, I came to truly believe Mama's version of the story, even if Mama didn't know the whole story. And I believed that if the yellowish-eyed Indian who was intent on doing me a certain amount of damage was indeed White Chaps, then he had played a trick on me by pretending to drown and was now somewhere safely in the Peace River Country doing whatever it was that Indians did.

I couldn't wait for the next issue of the *Sangudo Semi-Monthly* to appear in our mail slot at Fark General Store, but when the *Sangudo Semi-Monthly* did appear, what was in it was a distinct disappointment.

There was a little item in the third column on the second page that didn't provide any of the information I was anxious to be provided with, and the headline wasn't even about the murder itself.

TRACKING DOG A FAILURE, was how the headline read, and underneath it said there had been a murder on the Indian reserve north of Sangudo. It didn't name the Indian reserve, and only said the RCMP were searching for an Indian named Bartholomew White Chaps, who, after a night of drinking heavily, had shot his wife with a .22-calibre rifle and then attempted to shoot his father-in-law.

White Chaps, the article went on to say, had disappeared into wild terrain, and, in order to assist their officers, the RCMP had brought in their tracking dog, Abner, from Regina. However,

Abner, in spite of being given some of White Chaps's clothing to sniff, had simply run around in circles for an hour or so until he finally bogged down in a slough a mile or so south of the reserve.

The article ended by saying that Abner, the RCMP tracking dog, was being returned to Regina for further training.

Our subscription to the *Sangudo Semi-Monthly* continued even after we moved to the City of Edmonton at the end of August, and I scanned every single issue, hoping to see something about the search for, and hopefully the capture of, White Chaps, but nothing ever appeared either in the *Sangudo Semi-Monthly* or the *Edmonton Journal*, so I guess White Chaps was never captured, and I also guess that the file is still open, for the RCMP never close murder files and always get their man, though I imagine the files on White Chaps have come to gather a considerable amount of dust.